The Return of the Carter Boys:

The Carter Boys 2

The Return of the Carter Boys:

The Carter Boys 2

Desirée

URBAN BOOKS

www.urbanbooks.net

Urban Books, LLC
300 Farmingdale Road, NY-Route 109
Farmingdale, NY 11735

The Return of the Carter Boys: The Carter Boys 2
Copyright © 2018 Desirée

ISBN 13: 978-1-945855-51-1
ISBN 10: 1-945855-51-7

First Mass Market Printing November 2018
First Trade Paperback Printing May 2018
Printed in the United States of America

10 9 8 7 6 5 4 3 2 1

*This is a work of fiction. Any references or similarities
to actual events, real people, living or dead, or to real
locales are intended to give the novel a sense of reality.
Any similarity in other names, characters, places, and
incidents is entirely coincidental.*

Distributed by Kensington Publishing Corp.
Submit orders to:
Customer Service
400 Hahn Road
Westminster, MD 21157-4627
Phone: 1-800-733-3000
Fax: 1-800-659-2436

The Return of the Carter Boys:

The Carter Boys 2

by

Desirée

Granger

Something About Him

Noelle

"This is my jam!" My coworker Layla called out, raising her cup in the air as we moved through the packed crowd at the Gold Lounge. It was so much going on this weekend with the Classic and after parties that I'd had enough for one day. We'd been here for over an hour, and so far I'd been hit on by the creepiest men, or the sheisty-looking guys who probably approached every girl. It had been a rough week for me, my first week in Atlanta, so I thought a little night out would help me get over that. Now that I was here, smoke filled the air, drinks spilled on the floor, girls were wearing God knows what, men felt the need to touch up on me, and I'd had about enough.

Finding a decent spot to hang back at, we stood by ourselves as we enjoyed the music.

I looked down at my two-piece ensemble: royal blue skirt with the matching cropped long-sleeve top, hair with a slight curl to it, with my side bang on point.

"We gotta do this again next weekend!" Layla called out as I rolled my eyes with a smile.

"This might be my last!" I responded over the music just as a dark-skinned guy with a box cut walked over to me, looking like he had stepped out of an '80s music video. He looked me up and down in a dramatic fashion with a hand on his chin, smiling.

"Aye! You look even better up close with yo' sexy dark-skin ass!" he let out, chomping on gum. "What's yo' name, shawty?"

"Nigga, take yo' whack ass somewhere else!" Layla laughed with her head thrown back. "I can't believe you even approached her with that line."

"Wasn't nobody talking to yo' short, dumpling-looking ass!" he snapped as my eyes grew wide, looking from him to Layla. "My name is Ronny. What's yours, chocolate?"

"Apologize to her and maybe you'll find out," was all I said before moving farther down in disgust. I couldn't believe the nerve of some of these men here. I continued to move to the beat of the music, seeing Ronny and Layla going at it with her short self, finger all in his face as she rolled her neck.

"Damn, you sexy as fuck, guhl. What's yo' name?" a guy said, coming up behind me as he eyed my backside. He had a gold tooth in the front, braids going back—need I say more? "You look like one of them model bitches. You a model?"

"Girl!" Layla let out as she moved past the man, hand soaked. "I had to throw my drink in that nigga's face. He is too crazy."

"Are you serious?" I laughed, seeing the guy who tried to talk to me walk off. Layla was pure craziness, and I was sure he wanted no part of it. She moved her weave back off her shoulder as she continued to bounce to the music, occasionally twerking on me, trying to make me laugh.

"It's too many fine niggas in here to be getting hit on by the rejects," she let out, sipping through her straw. "Speaking of fine," she said, eyes zooming in on someone in particular. "This nigga has been staring you down the entire time."

"Who?" I asked, feeling my body tense as I looked around, but she grabbed my arm.

"Don't look, bitch. Just let me describe him before you freak him out." She laughed. "Tall, light skin, with some sexy-ass lips. Nigga looks like he could kill someone just by glancing at him. Definitely a trill nigga," she said as my mind immediately went to Shiloh.

I casually turned my head in her direction, and sure enough, it was him standing with a group of guys and a few girls, eyes on me. We locked eyes for a brief second as he tilted his head up toward me. I just smiled and did a small wave before looking back down at Layla, who was cheesing.

"Who is that?"

"That's my neighbor, the one I was telling you about," I said as I glanced back at him, seeing he hadn't taken his eyes off me. I hadn't spoken to him since the night I stayed at his house, but I was forever grateful. Still hesitant around him, but nonetheless grateful.

"Girl, he is fine as hell," she let out with a smack of her teeth. "And the niggas he's with look good too. Shit, tell him to come here."

"I'm not going to—"

"Fuck it," I said.

She started waving them over as my mouth dropped. I felt myself trying to hide within the people around us as she continued to frantically wave to him and his friends.

"Oh my God, Layla, what is wrong with you?" I laughed, turning around so that my back was turned.

"You already slept in this nigga's bed. Why are you so shy all of a sudden?" She laughed.

"Because we—"

"Shit! He's coming too!" She laughed as I dropped my head in embarrassment.

"What am I supposed to say? He doesn't talk to me when I'm home, barely talks at all. What am—"

"Heeey!" Layla greeted.

I turned, seeing Shiloh, and another guy walk over with his eyes on Layla. Shiloh said something to the guy before slapping hands with him.

"What up, li'l sexy?" the guy said to Layla, putting his arm around her neck as he walked her off.

Shiloh had deliberately told this man to occupy my friend. He stood next to me, acting shy and on mute. Looking him over in a brief second, I kept my smile hidden. Shiloh cleaned up well and smelled really good, considering we were in a club. He wore a red long-sleeve shirt that looked amazing against his light complexion, diamond stud in each ear, dark blue jeans with black high-top Gucci sneakers, fancy all-black watch, with his curly hair low and neat.

His low-lid eyes had a red tint as he licked his lips.

"Hi," I greeted, sticking my hand out for him to shake.

He just stared down at me, licking his lips, expression stone-cold mean. Clearing my throat, I thought of a way to break the awkward ice. "You enjoying yourself?"

"It's straight," Shiloh said in a deep voice. His eyes scanned the crowd like he was the protector of the club. "I just came through to support my brothers."

"That's nice." I smiled, looking at the group of guys he'd left behind. "Are those your brothers?"

"Nah," he said, looking back before pointing to the stage, where the Carter Boys were performing. I liked a few of their . . . Hold up.

"You're related to them?" I asked, shocked, remembering his last name was Carter. He nodded. "So, why you not up there singing and rapping?"

"Nah, not for me," he said with a small smile.

I could have seen pigs fly at that moment. I couldn't believe this man had just smiled at me. I tuned back into the song, bobbing my head just as Shiloh leaned in close to me, mouth against my ear.

"You probably the most beautiful girl I have ever seen."

My mouth dropped as he leaned back to see my expression, slow smile creeping on my face. I mouthed a *thank you* just as he leaned back in, a gentle hand on my lower back.

"Do you mind if I stay by your side for the rest of the night?"

My heart started to thump as I shook my head no. I knew it took all of him just to get those two sentences out, but for some reason, they meant the world to me. To hear him say it was completely different than to hear some random guy tell it to me.

"You got a ride to the crib?" he asked as he stood close to me, sipping on his drink.

"My friend is my ride. I left the car at home," I said, looking at him as he nodded. I watched his eyes watch everyone else. Girls had their eyes focused hard on Shiloh, who barely seemed to notice. Occasionally, they stepped up to him with the intention of talking, but he showed no interest.

Almost no guys walked up to me, though. Not even a glance. There was one brave soul who decided to try his luck as he walked up to me with his friends laughing behind him. I could see Shiloh, out of the corner of my eye, going completely still in mid-drink as he eyed the man approaching over the rim of his cup. Dude was tall, brown-skinned, with a little weight to him, wearing Lord knows what. It looked like borderline women's clothes with his jeans cut off and folded at the knees.

I didn't realize I had moved closer to Shiloh until I felt his body lightly bump mine. He kept his eyes hard on the guy, almost like he dared him to overstep.

"Aye, my homeboys and I were just looking at you, and no disrespect to you, bruh, but she is the sexiest dark-skin chick I've ever seen," the guy said, licking his lips hard at me. "I just wanted to get a closer look at yo' fine ass to make sure you were real."

"I'm real," I answered uneasily as Shiloh stepped up, putting his body slightly in front of mine. He didn't say anything, but it seemed like the guy understood as he held his hands up in surrender.

"You got it, bruh. I was just complimenting her," he said, backing up before turning to his friends.

Shiloh glanced at me as I put my hands on my hips, attitude lit.

"So, you're just going to claim me like that? No words, nothing? You barely speak when I do see you, but now all of a sudden it's no other man can talk to me now?" I pressed as he took a sip of his drink, giving me a side glance before nodding his head to the music. Unbelievable. He was just as crazy as the rest of the guys that approached me. I straightened up as I started looking for my friend. I was ready to go. He had just killed any moment, any vibe I might have been feeling for the night.

Gripping my clutch underneath my arm, I looked back at him, seeing his eyes were slowly scanning my body like it was a work of art before landing on my face.

"What, Shiloh?" I pressed, throwing my hand up in exasperation. "Why are you looking at me like that?" I didn't understand why the man was so quiet. Before he could say anything, a guy rushed over to us, muttering something in Shiloh's ear.

"Where he at?" Shiloh asked, putting his drink down as they both turned and walked off.

Just like that, I was alone again. Great. I started walking toward the exit as the lights popped back on, music cutting off. I could hear a loud commotion with the crowd, and I looked back, seeing two guys looking like they were about to get into a fight. Whatever.

I stepped outside, realizing I needed Layla to get home, but I had no idea where she was. Walking to where the car was parked, I realized another car had taken its place. *No, this bitch didn't just leave me here.* I quickly called her on my phone, but it went straight to voicemail.

"You cannot be fucking serious right now," I mumbled as I looked back at the club, seeing a few people walk out.

"Shit, I ain't fucking with that gun shit, nigga," I heard someone say as they rushed to their cars.

"Nigga was about to straight catch one. We would have all been sprayed, bruh."

"I can't believe black people act like they too hood to have a good time. Shit is so damn pointless! Stop the violence!" another girl ranted as she walked out with her friends.

I could hear the music cut back on, with the DJ talking on the mic. *Fuck it.* I attempted to call Layla again to see where she was, but I got no answer. *Ugh!* I walked back inside, moving through the thick crowd that was going in the opposite direction as I made my way back to the main floor.

"Aye," I heard a voice say, feeling a hand come to my lower back as I turned around. Shiloh stood there with a jacket on, keys in hand. "You ready?"

"Where did you tell your little friend to take my friend?" I pressed, arms crossing over my chest.

"I didn't tell that nigga shit. You ready?" he repeated, eyes cold, voice colder as he stared at me with no expression. I sighed as I followed him out of the club with at least fifteen-something people following behind him, moving only when he moved.

When I slipped inside his black Mustang, I felt myself about ready to explode. This guy had some nerve. Made my friend go away, wouldn't allow another guy to approach me, and yet he could barely open his mouth to me. What the hell? It didn't make sense. As soon as he pulled off, turning the music down, I crossed my legs in a cute manner, facing him, and let him have it.

"You have some damn nerve, Shiloh!" I snapped. His eyes grew wide, glancing at me before focusing back on the street. "We barely know each other, and you're acting like I'm your property. I never had a man treat me the way you're treating me now. When I was younger, my daddy always told me to be with a man that treats me as well, if not better, than he did. You have yet to show me any manners,"

I snapped. "You barely speak, you're always mean, not to mention you pointed a fucking gun to my head when all I was asking for was help. I mean . . ." I hesitated, thinking back. "Granted, you did take me in and made me two simple-ass sandwiches, but the way you're acting toward me is sooo cold, so mean, that I really don't know what to say to you." I waited for him to say something, anything. He just glanced at me with those low-set eyes, smirking to himself. "Are you serious right now? Like, serious? You think how I feel is funny?"

"I'm not yo' daddy, nor am I trying to be like that nigga, shawty," he said in a deep Southern-laced voice. "Just because I don't fucking speak and run my mouth like these bitch niggas you probably used to dealing with don't mean I don't know how to fucking conduct myself. Never pay attention to a man's words, shawty. I'm a man of action; words don't mean shit to me. All this talking you doing don't mean shit to me. If I want to make you my woman, I'm going to show you. I'm not going to tell you. If I want to fuck you, I'm going to show you. You understand where—"

"I give no fucks where you're coming from," I said, feeling my gritty nature come out. I really hated showing this side of myself. "I deserve respect because I have been nothing but nice to you. You have yet to show me respect since—fuck it," I snapped, throwing my hands up, seeing he was texting on his phone. He wasn't even paying attention to what I was saying.

We rode in silence for the next fifteen minutes until we pulled up to my house. I could feel myself about to start up all over again after having come up with different points to be made. "Don't even understand how you have friends," I mumbled, opening the door.

"I don't," he replied. "Don't need 'em."

"That wasn't a question for you to answer. Now you want to talk, but only when it's on some tit for tat shit. Get the fuck outta here," I snapped, slamming the door. "You are so rude and fucking inconsiderate!" I yelled through the window.

He got out of the car, closing the door behind him.

"You don't have to walk me to my door. I know how to get there just fine." I turned around, fumbling with my keys as my heels clicked against the dirty driveway with force. "Can't believe you act like I'm your fucking property because I spent one night in your

cold-ass bed. It doesn't work like that, Shiloh,"
I snapped, before mumbling to myself again
as I walked up the small steps to my porch.
"If you like someone, you tell them and show
them. Don't just force it on them like—" I
looked back, seeing he was walking up the
steps, hands in both pockets, smirking to
himself, which only pissed me off further.
"What the fuck is so funny?"

"You." He laughed outright. "You doing all
this arguing and screaming for what? You tiring
yourself out by doing that shit, like a puppy with
a tiny bark."

"Do you even know how to talk to women?" I
asked snidely, hands on my hips.

He stepped up to the porch, standing in front
of me as he looked down, while I looked up into
his expressionless face.

"You have got to be the weirdest man I ever
met. Maybe it's a good thing you don't have
friends, because you—"

He leaned down, and without further warning, kissed me on the lips. I let out a small gasp
of shock against his mouth before closing my
eyes, feeling his lips press against mine. I felt my
keys drop as my hands came to his sides, moving
closer to him as he deepened the kiss. Everything
in my body was saying *Yes! Oh Lord, yes.*

I felt his hand slip out of his pocket and slink around my waist, pulling me even closer. When he pulled back, our eyes locked.

"Can I take you out to lunch tomorrow?" he asked, face stone cold, yet the voice told me something different.

"Okay," I mumbled unintelligibly.

Tyree

"We are supposed to be out enjoying ourselves, looking for niggas. Instead, you got me sitting up here with yo' crying ass, looking at these sad-ass movies," Niya started, and I laughed, wiping my face.

It was three, maybe four in the morning on Sunday. I should have been out looking for new dick, but Ontrell ran through my mind like . . . I've been sad all damn day and night. He cheated on me and then finally came out and said he was going to continue to cheat on me. Niggas ain't shit; I swear they not. Love ain't shit either, because no matter how wrong he did me, I still loved him. Was I wrong? Was I crazy? So, I sat up in my apartment with my two main bitches—Tiffany's pregnant ass, and Niya, who was dressed for the club but decided to stick it out with me. We were on the couch, with blankets wrapped around us as we watched *Love & Basketball*, passing a blunt back and forth (minus the pregnant ho) and sharing a bottle.

"Girl, next week we going out. I promise. Trell ain't about to keep me down like this again. He got one night with me, and after all this sad shit, I'm done."

"You say that every time y'all break up," Tiffany said, and I rolled my eyes, tucking my feet in as I gripped my ankles. I only had on basketball shorts, so a bitch was cold, and this flimsy-ass blanket wasn't helping.

"This is the last time for real this time," I stated, grabbing the bag of chips. "I had my phone off all day, I haven't spoken to him. No rebound dick, no 'I'm sorry' sex. None of that. Honey, I'm done with them Carter boys. I can't handle it."

"Yeah, I hear they're turning up at the Gold Lounge as we speak," Niya said, reading a text message. "All you need to do is meet someone else. Trell thinks you're going to always be around, his backup nigga. When everyone else fails, he's got you to fall back on, and he's right. You take him back every time, but you need to stop doing that."

"I know, I know," I mumbled with a frustrated sigh. "It's a stupid bitch called Love that keeps making me take him back."

"Love need to get the fuck on then," Tiffany mumbled, mouth full of food, as we all laughed.

We fell into a comfortable silence as we watched the movie, with me glancing at my phone, dying to turn it on to see if he texted me or left a message. *Fuck it*. I grabbed my phone without them noticing and went to the back where my room was. I lived comfortably in a one-bedroom apartment, decorated to a T, closet fit for a king—although most of this shit in there was Trell's. We didn't have the same style, so we rarely shared clothes, but one side was his, the other was mine. His shoes took up most of the floor space.

I went into the closet, sitting up against the plastic shelf that held our jewelry, and turned my phone on. Waiting, all I kept hearing was, "That's why I cheat on you: because I can! I've been doing it, and I'm going to keep doing it." It was the only thing that kept playing in my mind on repeat. As soon as the phone cut on, I waited for the voice messages to come up, but nothing. There were a few emails from my clients, a few text messages from my boos and bitches, but nothing from my man. We were really done. I dropped my phone, feeling my body go numb as I let the tears fall.

"Damn, Ontrell!" I let out, hitting the hanging clothes. "Fuck is wrong with you? I'm the best thing that ever happened to yo' sorry ass. Nobody knew who the fuck you were before me."

Suddenly, my phone went off. I looked down at the screen. His older brother Anthony was calling.

"Hello?" I answered, trying to clear my throat. Didn't want nobody knowing I was crying.

"Aye, come get this nigga, bruh. Passed the fuck out crying over yo' ass. Come up here and get him. My baby mama keep coming at me."

"Don't call that fuck nigga!" I heard Trell yell out, and I rolled my eyes. "Slashing my tires like a bitch. You a bitch, Tyree! Might as well fuck a real bitch."

"You at home, Anthony?" I asked, slipping on Trell's Jordans and hoodie. I tuned out Trell because all he was going to do was rant. When he got drunk, that's what he did.

"Yeah, we just got here. He was too much for the club, so come get him, and stop and get some diapers."

"Nigga, you must have lost yo' damn mind," I said, hanging up the phone. *Get some diapers? Nah-uh, boo.*

I walked out of my room, grabbing my keys. "Aye! We gotta go! I gotta go pick up Trell's drunk ass."

"What?" the girls shrieked as I opened the front door, waiting on them to walk out.

"Don't ask, but I'd rather him here than out on the street, so come on. Y'all need to go home anyway."

"You better not take his ass back," Niya warned as I closed the door with a lock.

"I won't. I promise," I stated.

They got in their cars, going in one direction as I drove off in another.

Anthony didn't live too far from me, but I did stop by the gas station, buying those cheap diapers they sold, and continued on my way, reaching his place. I honked the horn, pulling up to the curb just as the front door opened. I could see Anthony holding Trell, helping him walk down the driveway to my car.

"You want him in the back seat?" Ant asked as I reached back, opening the door.

"Lay him down right here," I demanded, looking at Trell as he lay back in the seat, eyes halfway open, breath smelling like shit, body smelling like sweat, and shit all in his dreads. "What the fuck kind of party y'all performed for?" I asked, handing him the bag from the store.

"Nah, it wasn't even like that. He just had too much, did too much. Whatever the fuck y'all got going on again, fix that shit before he kill himself over you."

"It's not me! He's the one that cheats on me, Anthony. Stop taking his—"

"I don't give a fuck, Ty. Y'all need to either stay the fuck away from each other or get that shit together."

"Tell yo' punk-ass brother that, nigga. Miss me with that shit," I snapped, stepping on the gas. I didn't have time to hear no shit like "Fix it." What the fuck am I fixing? I didn't know it was broken until I saw the damn pieces.

I struggled to get him back up to my apartment, since he decided he wanted to fight me the whole way. When I got him to the room, I made him sit in the tub, stripped him down, and turned the shower on. Hopefully that would sober him up a little bit. I already had my loaf of bread waiting on the bathroom counter as he laid back on the tub, water hitting his cut brown-chocolate body, dick hard for no reason.

"Fuck you staring at, nigga?" he asked as our eyes met. "Shit don't belong to you no more."

"Whatever, Trell. You can have yo' ho-ass dick," I snapped, crossing my legs as I sat on the closed toilet lid. He stared at me with those mean eyes, dreads falling everywhere, with those sexy chocolate lips that could do no wrong. My man was the finest thing next to me—well, my ex man.

"Cut this water off," he groaned, wiping his face.

I reached over, cutting the water off, seeing he was still in and out, but at least able to have a conversation. I got up to get a slice of bread and handed it to him. When I say the nigga smacked my hand away? I was done.

"You know what?" I started, grabbing the whole loaf of bread. "Fuck you, Trell. I didn't have to pick yo' sorry ass up from yo' brother's house. I should have let his baby mama put yo' ass out the damn house!" I snapped, throwing the loaf at him, smacking him hard in the face before walking out. "Got me fucked up as usual. Don't even know why I do half the shit I do for yo' punk ass." I continued to rant as I stripped down and walked to the living room to lay on the couch. I didn't even want to sleep in the same bed we shared. I didn't want to see him; didn't want him to see me. No talking, no nothing. I was done. I pulled the blanket over me and continued to watch my movie.

"Hope you fucking slip and bust yo' ass!" I yelled out before laying back down.

"Fuck you!"

"Nigga, you can talk that shit all the way out the fucking door, Trell. I'm done with you. Get yo' shit and go."

I could hear him yelling, but I turned the TV up, knowing he was going to hit me with the '"Who pays the bills? Who does this; who does that?" *Well, who cheats, who lies countless times, again and again? Not me. Not I, bum nigga.*

I continued to drown him out with the TV until eventually, I felt secure enough to fall asleep. I hated going to sleep angry. I really did. The headache, the waking up still mad? I hated that shit, but a bitch was tired.

It wasn't until I felt a strong wind walk past me, smelling like weed, that I opened up one eye. I could already see daylight trying to peek through the dark sky as I watched Trell turn the TV off. He was in his boxers, dreads tied up, black socks up high, cleaning up the living room, fixing pillows on the chair, adjusting my fur rug, and wiping down the small coffee table. I just watched him smoking the last bit of his blunt while taking plates to the kitchen.

When he came back, he got on the small couch with me, slipping his tall ass underneath the small blanket, laying in the opposite direction.

"You love me?" he asked, blowing smoke out through his nose as I looked at him.

Here we go.

I said nothing; just stared at him.

"So, you don't love me no more?"

I turned my head, snatching the covers from him and closing my eyes. I could feel him move as he grabbed my ankles, tickling my feet.

"Ontrell!" I laughed, trying to kick him. "You need to stop. I'm serious!"

"Told you about having these funky-ass feet on my couch anyway," he let out, playfully running his fingers up against the base of my foot. I nearly pissed on myself I was laughing so hard.

"Trell, I'm not playing with yo' ass!" I laughed, snatching my feet away from his grasp. He sat up, trying to lay over my body, attacking the side of my face with kisses.

"I love you, and I'm sorry," he said against my ear.

"You ain't sorry."

"Yes, I am. I'm going to do better."

"You say that shit every time, nigga," I snapped, trying to push him off me, but he held on tighter.

"You love me?"

"You know I do," I mumbled, hating that I even still felt like he was my everything. I looked at him, seeing he was looking at me, blunt still in his hand. I decided to reach out and take it, taking a long pull on it before blowing smoke directly in his face.

"Aw, you ain't shit for that, nigga." He laughed softly before kissing me. "Can you come back to the room?"

"Nope. I can't sleep in there with you no more."

He let out a sigh before sitting back, taking some of the blanket.

"Well, then I'm staying out on this small-ass couch with you, because I can't sleep without you."

Text Message Sent

Tia

"How you feeling?" Porscha asked as she lay on the bed next to me. Everyone was out partying, while I sat my ass in the room, looking up everything I could on babies and being pregnant: what to expect, how to care for it, what to eat while you're pregnant.

"Sick as fuck," I said, looking at my phone. "I've been trying to figure out whether or not I should tell Jahiem I'm keeping this baby."

"Well, I think you should. Regardless of how you feel about him, he has a right to know his own seed is going to be birthed into the world. Did you want his help?"

"No! Fuck no," I spat. "I don't even want to see him again."

"So, just tell that nigga, 'Look, I'm having the baby. You don't have to be here to help me raise it. You can continue on with your life.' You know he's going to expect you to ask him for money, right?"

"I don't want it. He can keep that too. I can do this shit all by myself. I been looking for a job now. I got an interview at McDonald's next week."

"What, bitch? McDonald's? You can do better," she let out as I laughed. "But yeah, you need to tell that nigga. Matter of fact, hand me the phone. I'd rather you tell him now than him seeing yo' pregnant ass later on. Niggas like him don't take surprises well." She went through my phone and set it up to where she was about to text him.

"Hi, this is Tia, the girl you got pregnant. I just want to say thank you for taking me to the clinic, but I decided I couldn't get the abortion. Nothing changes, nigga. I still don't—" She read out loud, texting as she tried to catch up to what she was saying. "I still don't want you in my, or the baby's, life. I don't need your money, and you can delete my number after this message. Bye." She looked at me and asked, "How does that sound?"

"I can't tell him, not until I'm completely sure I'm having this baby," I said with a sigh as she smacked her teeth.

"Girl, you already trying to get a job, thinking about saving up so you can move out. You already thinking like a single parent. Might as well."

"Well, I don't want to scare him. Don't send it. Not yet. Give me another week," I said.

She was silent as I looked at her, eyes glued to the phone. I glanced at the screen, seeing the message was already sent.

"Porscha!"

"I didn't mean to do it!" She laughed as I grabbed the phone, trying to literally bring the fucking message back with my mind.

Shit, shit, shit! Fuck!

"Bitch, I oughta whoop yo' fucking ass now," I snapped, nearly pushing her dumb ass off my bed. "I can't believe you."

"He might not even read the message. Nigga is probably drunk as fuck, higher than a kite, and living it up right now. Probably won't see it until tomorrow. That gives you enough time to get a new number."

"Bitch, I don't want a new number. Girl, I can't even deal with you. I'm pregnant, and I'm tired."

"You not even showing!" she said, and we both laughed. "Don't use that excuse yet with yo' ho ass."

"Whatever, trick." I laughed. I loved my best friend. Looking back at the phone, I sighed. Well, the nigga was going to find out eventually.

"Don't even worry about it. I'll see if my fertile ass can get pregnant by my nigga so we can have babies together," she said. I looked at her, knowing she was playing. At least I hoped she was.

So, as you know, the only thing on my mind was that text message. I even shut my phone off because I was afraid of the response, the reaction—or no reaction and no response. Either way, I was nervous as hell. I wasn't trying to leave this bed, you know, early Sunday morning, TV on, watching BET Inspiration because I needed that in my life right now. I needed to hear the Word or something, because it seemed like everything was working against me.

I rolled onto my side, looking at my phone charging on the floor, scared to touch that bitch. If I didn't see nothing from this nigga, I told myself, that was him telling me he didn't give a fuck. Not that I cared, but him telling me he was not trying to be a part of this baby's life? I didn't even want to be a part of this baby's life, but I couldn't bring myself to get an abortion, so here I was, about to really try to raise this child. I reached over, grabbing the phone off the charger, and cut it on.

"Lord Jesus," I mumbled with my eyes closed, hearing the phone load up. I could feel my stomach hurting like I was in for another round of throwing up.

Looking around my room, I thought about this being my last semester here. I needed my own place. My parents weren't going to let me in the house with a baby on the way, not while I was supposed to be finishing my degree. I looked down at my stomach, thinking about the potential life that was growing, before my phone repeatedly started to vibrate back to back. *Shit.*

I saw text messages from my friends who had found out I was pregnant, congratulating me on the new life, and then I saw Jahiem's messages, all in caps. He was pissed, to say the least. Looking at the time, I saw that these were sent to me about an hour ealier. It was going on eleven o'clock now.

HOW CAN U KEEP THE FUCKING BABY
WITHOUT ASKING ME? WAT ABOUT WAT I WANTED?
U A FUCKING HOE ASS BITCH WALKING AROUND TRYNA
SAY THAT SHIT IS MINE! IM NOT HELPING U TAKE CARE
OF THAT FUCK SHIT! DNT ASK ME FOR NOTHING, DON'T
CALL ME. LOSE MY FUCKING NUMBER WIT YO HOE ASS.

Next message:

AYE, U UP?
ANSWER THE FUCKING PHONE! Y U GOT THIS
SHIT OFF AFTER U TELLING ME U KEEPING MY BABY?
I BET U FUCKING SOME FUCK NIGGA NOW TRYING
TO PUT THAT BABY ON TO HIM.

I continued to scroll down, reading as my mouth dropped. I was nearly sweating bullets, heart beating as I read this bullshit. This nigga had straight lost his mind.

I KNOW THAT BABY AINT MINE BCUZ U
ALREADY LIED TO ME TALKIN ABOUT U GOT
THE ABORTION! IT WAS PROBABLY UR PLAN ALL
ALONG TO KEEP THAT SHIT! ANSWER THIS DAMN
PHONE! I DNT EVEN KNW WHAT THE FUCK YO NAME IS!

"Nigga, you know my name," I retorted as I saw an incoming message from him. I could do him one better. I pressed CALL CONTACT and waited as the phone rang. Nigga wanted to cuss me out on the Lord's day? Oh, no, boo.

"Hello?" He answered, and my head cocked back. I looked at the phone before putting it on speaker.

"Nigga, first of all. Don't answer like you didn't just go the fuck off on me through a text."

"Nah, bruh! You doing stupid shit. I tried calling you. Yo' scary ass wants to send me some fuck shit like that and then cut yo' phone off. Why are you keeping this baby? Even if that shit is mine, I'm not ready to be a fucking parent."

"You don't have to be, Jahiem. I'm not asking you to be one. I was just letting you know what I planned on doing. I already got this shit figured out. I can do it by myself. I don't need your help."

"You not getting this shit," he said as he turned the radio down in the background, mumbling to himself, slick trying to cuss me out under his breath.

"Nigga, speak up!"

"Be outside in five," he said before hanging up.

"I don't want to see you!" I screamed out to no one as I threw my phone down. I threw on some sweats on top of my shorts and a hoodie, brushed my teeth real quick, and wrapped my hair up again. I looked rough: bags underneath my eyes, swollen face from lack of sleep because I was too worried about this bitch nigga here. I grabbed my keys and walked out of my room, seeing Jordyn going into Jade's room, closing the door.

I walked out of the apartment and headed downstairs, feeling my phone vibrate from him calling. *Damn, nigga, I'm coming. Shit.*

I pushed open the glass doors and saw him standing, posted up on the hood of his red Camaro, locs pulled back into a ponytail, with his hands in his camouflage jacket, gray hoodie underneath, with black straight-leg jeans and gray-and-black Jordans. His almond-shaped eyes were looking pulled back as he stared at me, pissed.

I stood in front of him with my arms crossed, feeling ugly as shit, but I didn't give two fucks about impressing this nigga.

"So, you don't see nothing wrong with having this baby without asking me if I was okay with it?"

"Nigga, you act like you're the one carrying it," I snapped with my hand thrown up in the air.

"I'm not, but that shit is mine as much as it's yours. Well, hold up," he said, hand on his chin as if he was thinking, trying to be funny. "If you do have this baby, best believe we getting a DNA test."

"I ain't getting shit, nigga. It's yours."

"I don't want this baby!" Jahiem cried out. "I don't want to be a daddy at fucking twenty-seven."

"Nigga, I'm not trying to be a mother."

"So get rid of it!" Jahiem yelled as if that would solve all the problems. "I don't want this child. I don't want to have to deal with you for the rest of my life if it is mine, and—"

"I didn't want to have sex with you," I said, shutting all this shit up. "But that shit happened."

He stared at me then dropped his head before turning around to face the car.

"Fuuuuuck!" he screamed out, slamming his fist down on the roof of his car as he held his head down. I just stood there, silent, watching and waiting. "Can't believe this is happening to me."

"It's not happening to you, Jahiem," I let out. "Like, I don't want you near me while I'm pregnant, and I damn sure don't want you around when the baby is here. You can continue to live your life. I got a job interview at McDonald's next week. I can make my own money and finish school to get my degree to get a better job. Nigga, I don't need you. You understand?" I said as he turned to look at me.

"I'm not that kind of dude," was all he said, barely above a mumble as he pulled out his phone. "You really keeping this kid?"

"I am," I stated determinedly, watching him look me in the eye hard before unlocking the doors to his car.

"So, I guess we got to figure out the next step then," he said, and my eyes lit up. I was not expecting that. "I'm going to help you until this baby is born, we get a DNA test, and if this mothafucka turns out not to be my kid?" He didn't say anything, just gave me a look like I should already know what was going to happen next.

"Nigga, I'm not scared of you," I retorted with an eye roll.

"You should be," he stated, eyes never leaving mine. "I've been locked up before. I have no problem going back. Remember that. Get in the fucking car," he demanded as he slipped inside the driver's seat.

"I'm not—"

"I'm hungry, I got a fucking hangover, and I want to talk more about this dumb-ass shit you doing, so get in the car," he said again, cutting the engine on.

"I'm not going nowhere looking like this," I let out as I turned to walk back to my building.

"Who the fuck cares what you look like? Just get in the car! Shit, what is yo' name?"

"Tia!" I walked back inside and headed straight for my room, getting the shower going.

When I walked back out, it had to be thirty minutes or so later. Maybe an hour. I thought he would have left, but he was sitting in his car on the phone, running his mouth. Of course, you know, despite me hating this nigga, I had to stunt, so I walked out in my Sunday best, a cute, dark-blue long shirt with the white stripe on the sleeves. On the front it said *Urban Chic*. I wore it like a dress because it was that long. My natural hair was out, so I undid my twist, letting the curly fro run wild, feeling so afro cute that day. It was usually not my style, but I dressed according to my hair. Makeup was light and cute, I carried a cute tote bag, matching chucks, and I was ready to go. I peeped Jahiem giving me a look-over before shifting his eyes elsewhere. *Yeah, nigga, I saw it.*

As I slipped inside the comfortable seats, he closed his door and backed out.

"Yeah, let me hit you back, bruh," he said before hanging up as he looked me over.

I rolled my eyes, not wanting to say a word. I just tried to keep myself from throwing up all over this nigga's car. Even I had to admit it was nice. Shit looked like the inside of a race car, sleek and futuristic-like.

"Where you trying to eat at?" he asked.

"I'm not eating, so I don't know."

"Fuck you mean you not eating? Now that you're pregnant, don't you think you got to eat something? What y'all women be saying? I'm eating for two?"

"I don't like throwing up. Shit hurts when I do it."

"So go to the fucking doctor and let them give you something for it. I'm not understanding the problem," he retorted, getting on the highway.

It grew quiet. Too quiet. I didn't want to respond, because I didn't feel like I needed to. He had a way of coming off as a know-it-all. People like that need to hear themselves talk. *Run that mouth, nigga. I'm not running with ya.*

"Waffle House," I let out suddenly, and he glanced at me. I hadn't eaten there in forever. When I used to club hard as fuck, we would always stop at Waffle House on the way back.

"That's where you want to go?" he asked, and I nodded. "Shit, we probably passed about three or four of them mothafuckas."

"I can eat a little bit," I said, holding my stomach, feeling it turn. "I'm supposed to eat light food. Nothing heavy."

"When do you start showing?" he asked, glancing at my stomach. I shrugged. "How the fuck you even know you really pregnant?"

"Nigga, would you just drive? I had a checkup when I went to the clinic. They confirmed I was pregnant."

"Just making sure. You already lied once to me."

"Like you didn't lie to get me to sleep with y—"

"Look, if you're going to keep bringing that shit up, realize now I'm not sorry for that night, okay?" he said, looking at me with a hard glare. "I don't give a fuck what you think. You came in that house wanting to get fucked. You got fucked by me, and it was the best you ever had, so—"

"It was not the best I ever had, so chill, bruh," I said with a sarcastic laugh. He tucked his lower lip in as he glanced at me with a knowing look. "I've had far better."

"Yeah, I bet," he mumbled, getting off at the nearest exit.

"Whatever, nigga," I said, waving him off as I started texting Porscha, telling her what the fuck was going on at this very moment. She wasn't going to believe this shit.

When we pulled up to Waffle House, I could already see it was going to be hell trying to get a table. Getting out of the car, I fixed my fro before closing the door, seeing he was just watching me with a tired look.

"Why you wear so much makeup? And why you so into how you look?" he questioned with a disgusted look on his face.

"I'm not. Why are you so concerned with how I look?"

"I'm not. Believe me, I'm not." He laughed. "I get badder bitches than you without makeup on an off day. I hate that cake shit."

I stayed quiet as I checked my face in my compact mirror before walking around the car to walk with him inside. I already knew from the previous time we were together that he had an issue with makeup. He was probably into the natural-looking girls who didn't shave and shit. *Whatever, nigga. Not my problem.*

I didn't know what the smell was, maybe it was the cigarette smoke or the smell of grease, but I immediately gripped my stomach and went the quickest route to the bathroom, barely making it to the toilet before I threw up.

"I can't do this," I mumbled, feeling tears about to come down as I wiped my mouth. What the fuck was I thinking, keeping this damn baby? I could barely handle this morning sickness, and I was just beginning.

"Aye," I heard Jahiem sound off, knocking on the stall door as my eyes grew wide.

"Nigga, this is the ladies' bathroom. Get out!" I shrieked before feeling another round coming up. I gripped the stall walls as I coughed up the aftermath, feeling my kinky hair falling in my face.

"I just came in here to see what the fuck you wanted to order."

"I'm not eating!"

"I swear on my mama, shawty, you—"

I let out another round, crying out as I gripped my stomach. This couldn't be normal morning sickness. I definitely needed to go to the doctor on this one, like tomorrow. This didn't seem like anything I'd read online.

The stall door opened, and Jahiem came in, closing it behind him.

"Shit," he hissed as he came to the side of me, with me immediately gripping his jeans as I kneeled over the toilet, spitting and coughing up whatever was left. My chest was heaving as he took my bag, putting it on his shoulder.

"So worried about looking cute. This shit is getting in your hair," he snapped as he pulled my hair back.

"Is there a man in here?" Someone asked hesitantly.

I was just about to answer, but Jahiem cut in, "Mind yo' fucking business!"

The woman gasped, and the door closed shut.

Holding on to my hair as I puked out the last bit, he dug in my purse and pulled out a hair tie, attempting to tie my hair up. I flushed the toilet and wiped my mouth. My eyes were swollen red.

"You gotta go to the doctor tomorrow and see what the fuck is this shit. My brother got three baby mamas, and theirs wasn't as bad as this."

"I know," I mumbled as I took my bag from him.

The Fight

Jordyn

"Homecoming weeeeek!" someone yelled out as the crowd of students went crazy. Everyone was standing outside in front of the student center late Monday night with all the Greeks of the yard represented. "This week, we are having a party every single night on Greek Row! Y'all come out, show some love!"

"Aye!" Trent yelled out as he kept his arm around Jade, who was loving every bit of the attention. "Private after party at the red house after the game! You already know what time it is, beautiful ladies."

I rolled my eyes as I continued to maneuver through the growing crowd with books in my arms. I could hear the whispers of people talking about me in between the announcements as I moved.

"That's the girl that was with Jodie at the party," someone whispered as I pushed my glasses up.

"Aye yo, Jordyn!" a guy with dreads called out.

I squinted my eyes hard as I looked at him and his friends, wondering who the hell they were in the first place before I kept moving.

"Ah, bruh, that was her at the party in the white dress. She was looking bad as fuck Saturday night, nigga," another said as I locked eyes with one guy who was staring me down like I was naked.

I couldn't handle this much unwanted attention. I could hear the sounds of men barking as a group of guys all wearing gold boots rushed up to the crowd, tongues hanging out, just as I passed by them. One in particular did a double take as he looked at me, smiling.

"Aye, you was that girl at the party in the white?" he said as he stopped in front of me. I felt so short standing next to him. He was tall and wide, with a purple Polo hat on, purple shirt, and gold spray-painted boots.

"Yeah?" I questioned, pushing my glasses up. I was back to my basic style of wardrobe: jeans, hoodie, and sneakers. Nothing fancy, no name brands, none of that. My hair was tossed up in a tight bun on my head.

"Damn, I don't know how I let you slip by my sight, ma," he let out, licking his lips as he looked me over.

Oh, fuck no. This guy had to be three times the average man's size. I just moved nervously past him, but he grabbed my arm.

"Hey, we throwing something small at the house later on tonight. You should stop by. Real talk, not even on no sex shit, ma. You got all the brothers wanting to see about you, so I know you got a million niggas coming at you."

"I don't—"

"Nah, it's cool," he said, cutting me off. I stopped myself from rolling my eyes. "Just stop by, ma. You was sexy as fuck at that party, baby," he continued as more of his brothers came up.

"Oohh, shit! This is her, the chick that's with the Carter Boys? Damn! You was looking good as fuck at that party, shawty!" another said as more people started to surround me, completely ignoring the Greeks.

I could barely get a word in as guys started asking me questions about music, getting their own mixtapes to the Carter Boys, and asking if I was sleeping with Jodie Carter. I almost didn't even recognize the name before remembering that was Elijah's middle name. I could barely get my phone out fast enough as guys started reciting their numbers to me, all speaking at once.

"Nigga, chill!" one guy snapped to another, putting his hand in front of the guy to push him back. "I don't want her like that. I'm trying to make moves in the industry. You can have her."

"Bruh, do that shit on yo' own then, nigga. Aye, make sure you call me," another guy said to me as I took down another number.

I was handed CDs, guys writing their numbers down on paper, and invites to parties. Girls wanted in on the action too, suddenly wanting me to hang out with them. It was like I had become popular based off one night alone. The crowd surrounding me grew bigger as the crowd surrounding the Greeks grew smaller with each passing second. I was dubbed the girlfriend of the Carter Boys. The girlfriend of Jodie Carter. When they started to get a little too packed for my liking, with me dropping some of my things, I could feel my anxiety about to take over. I felt like a mouse surrounded by lions, with no one hearing me for me. All they remembered was that night at the party. *Girl in the white dress! Girl in the white dress!*

"Shit, nigga, why the fuck would she waste time on you if she got that nigga Jodie?" one guy snapped on another as they started arguing.

I looked around for any familiar face before locking eyes with Trent, who made his way over, wearing his dress shirt, pants, and bowtie. His hazel eyes were bright, with his bag strapped across his body.

"Aye yo, move! Move out the way!" he called out to everyone as he wrapped an arm around my neck, pulling me close to his body. "Y'all need to get the fuck on!"

"Yo, get at me, Jordyn!" one guy called out, following Trent to open space as we walked.

"Trent! Tell—"

"I ain't telling her shit!" he yelled out, looking back. "Hey, my bad about all of this. I told Elijah that this shit was going to happen. You going back to the room, right?" I nodded, still unable to speak. "Cool. I'll walk with you. Got some shit in Jade's room I need to get anyway."

We walked back to the apartment in silence. I could feel my lower body throbbing. Don't know why, but that physical attraction to Trent was definitely there, regardless of whether he felt the same way. He was more my type than Elijah in all aspects. We were more alike than Elijah and I anyway.

"So, you like my brother?" Trent asked as we crossed over to the parking lot leading up to my building. The streetlights were on, beaming down on the cars as I looked up at him with a small smile.

"I do," I said, shrugging, trying to keep my conversation minimal.

"Nah, don't play that cool shit with me. You probably in love with that nigga," Trent joked as we walked inside the warm building, heading straight for the stairs. "I never seen him act like that with a girl the way he does with you. So, either y'all on some ol' lovey-dovey shit, or the sex is just that good," he joked as I glanced at him, no smile, with a hint of arousal.

"My sex is just that good," I stated.

We stared at each other for a split second before I looked away. I should not have been looking at my roommate's boyfriend that way, but I couldn't help it.

We walked up to the apartment in silence as I opened the door. It was pitch black in there, smelling like incense. I set my stuff down on the table, popping the lights on as he walked back to Jade's room. No one was there, just us.

Walking to my room, I immediately stripped down to my shirt and panties as I dug through my closet looking for a fresh towel. I was definitely in for the rest of the night. Pushing my glasses up, I pulled out a nice black towel before almost screaming in fear when I saw Trent standing at the doorway. I was pretty sure I had closed my door.

"What are you doing?" I asked, wrapping the towel around my waist, hazel eyes getting heavy as he stared me down.

"I was just about to . . ." He dropped his head with a slow shake. "Fuck. I can't believe I let Elijah get to you before me."

"What?" I flipped, with my face scrunched up.

"I just . . . you too good for that nigga."

"Kind of like how you're too good for Jade?" I pressed. Any attraction I felt for him at that moment disappeared when he mentioned his brother. Yeah, I was too good for Elijah, but I still took offense to that on his behalf.

"That's different. I know Elijah, and I know how that nigga is. You can do better," he stated, licking his lips as he looked me over. "Best believe if I wasn't with Jade, you would have been mine, had I known you would look the way you did that night."

I felt my body go numb at that statement before feeling disgusted. "Get the fuck out of my room," I snapped, and his eyes grew in confusion. "Now! Get out! Don't ever fucking talk to me again, or I'm going to tell Jade you tried to hit on me."

"Fuck you getting mad for? It's the truth and you know it! Don't tell me you not attracted to me like that," he let out. "Elijah don't know what to do with a girl with smarts and beauty like you. That's all I'm saying."

"Get out!"

"Whateva, man." He threw his hands in the air and walked out with a small laugh. "You know it's true. That's why you mad."

"No!" I snapped, following behind him. "I'm mad because for once I thought you would have been different, but you're just like every other fuck nigga that was out on the yard coming at me! Had you known I would look the way I did that night?" I flipped, feeling my Northern roots hit hard. "You egotistical piece of shit! Elijah was the only, and still is the only person that doesn't care what the fuck I look like."

"Because he will fuck anything moving. I know my own brother." He laughed, still not understanding my point. "You a grown-ass woman. No reason why you should be looking the way you look now, Jordyn. All I'm saying. If you take offense to that, my bad, but I keep it one hundred every time, baby."

"Get out," I repeated, rushing to the front door to open it. There stood Jade, who was just about to put her key in when she saw the two of us. "He can't come in here anymore, Jade," I stated, feeling bold as hell.

Her head cocked back, honey gold locks bouncing as her face turned to pure confusion. "And who the fuck is you to tell me my nigga can't come here?" she pressed, hand on her hip as she set her stuff down on the table. "What the fuck happened? And why the fuck are you walking around in yo' underwear in front of him in the first place?"

I looked down, seeing the towel dropped to the floor. I had not even realized it.

"She mad because I told her the truth, baby," Trent said, trying to downplay it.

"He can't come back here. As your roommate, and hopefully a friend, you can respect my wishes," I stated, arms crossed over my chest.

She just looked at me before bursting out into laughter. "Jordyn, get the fuck outta here. We cool, but we not friends like that, ma," she let out, locs bouncing with every movement. "My nigga is going to continue to come over here, and if you got a problem with it, then move the fuck out. You think you big shit now that you're the girl everyone wants?"

"I never said—"

"Clearly that's how you fucking acting though, right?" she snapped, voice getting louder as I backed up. "Put some fucking clothes on around my nigga. Now that I know how yo' ho ass really get down, I'm not so sure I'm comfortable with you staying here period."

Before I could even respond, Tia walked in with her friend Porscha. When she saw all of us near the door, her hateful eyes immediately went to mine in disgust. Every night it was the same thing with her: pick on Jordyn, fuck with Jordyn. Well, Elijah told me one day I was going to snap and go off on everyone. I was starting to feel like that might just happen tonight.

"What the fuck is going on?" Tia asked, putting her bag down on the crowded dining room table.

"She talking about Trent can't come over here." Jade smirked, and I looked at Trent, eyes wide like he didn't expect it to take this turn. "She think she cute because she fucking with one of the Carter Boys. Suddenly she feel like she's untouchable."

"Hold up, hold up!" Tia laughed slowly as she stepped to me. "Who you fucking with? What are y'all talking about?"

"You were the bitch in the white dress everyone was talking about?" Porscha yelled out with a laugh. "Bitch! She's the one that's been fucking Elijah!"

The moment I heard his name, I felt my body go completely numb. Tia's facial expression could have killed me on the spot. I didn't know if something triggered in her mind, but without warning, she hauled off and hit me dead in my face. Suddenly, it felt like everything happened in slow motion.

I can't fight to save my life, but I started wildly swinging at anyone, hearing Trent yell just as I felt a hand jerk at my hair, pulling me down to the kitchen floor. I was screaming out in pain as I felt my face get beat and hair get pulled, ripping out of my scalp. I started kicking hard, trying to block my face or push whoever it was off me. It felt like ten people on me as I cried out. I felt my body get jerked in different directions as another set of hands started pounding at the side of my face, while another got me in the face, throat, and chest.

"Please!" I cried. "Stop! I'm sorry for whatever I—" I felt my head get pulled up by my hair before being slammed back down to the floor hard. I cried out again, tasting blood, feeling bald and helpless.

"Aye! Jade! Chill!" Trent yelled, trying to grab her away from me. "Shit! Shit! Yo, y'all gotta stop! Fuck is wrong with y'all?"

"Bitch! Who told you you could fuck my nigga?" Tia yelled in anger, voice shaking as she hit me again. "Hold her legs still, Porscha!"

"I got you, bitch! Get her ass!" Porscha cheered, grabbing my legs.

"Yo, I need some help!" Trent yelled out.

I could feel myself going in and out of consciousness before suddenly feeling hands and bodies being pulled away from my body. I couldn't move. I couldn't speak or open my swollen eyes.

"Damn, she is fucked up!" someone let out. "Yo, where my phone at?"

I lay there, hearing the voices, hearing Trent go off on Jade, who yelled back, and hearing what sounded like camera phones going off. I heard it all. There was nothing I could do about it. None of this would have happened if I didn't go to that stupid-ass party. Nobody knew who I was before all of this, and now everyone was going to know who I was because of this.

When all was said and done, with the help of some students, I was taken to the clinic before being taken back to my room. Tia was still upset, going off at the mouth, and Jade was nowhere to be found. Having left my phone in the room, I saw where Elijah had called me seventeen times, text messaged back to back, wanting to know what had happened and who did what. Rita called, already having heard what happened, and my parents called, more likely to ask if I was coming home for the holidays. My face was swollen red, eyes barely open, bruises on my chest and sides, and lip busted. I looked unrecognizable.

Feeling tears come down, I dialed Elijah's number. He answered on the first ring.

"Who did that shit?" he asked immediately.

"I don't . . . " I mumbled off, realizing it hurt to open my mouth. "Elijah," I cried softly into the phone. "Please come get me."

"Aw, Jordyn, don't cry, baby. Please don't do that shit," he begged. "I won't be back in town until Friday. Fuck!" he snapped suddenly. "I can send someone to get—"

"Nooo," I moaned, crying harder into the pillow. I was in so much pain. My body was sore, face was swollen, mouth felt like every time I opened it to speak, a million trucks just rammed into me. My head was on fire from where they pulled my hair. I could see the clumps on the floor, and blood still on my clothes. I needed to be away from this place. I was afraid to sleep here at night, afraid of what they might do to me.

"Yo, have yo' shit together. I'm going to see if I can fly in tomorrow morning, a'ight?"

"K," I mumbled, hanging up.

The very next morning, Elijah came through for me. More than came through, actually. I had the door unlocked for him as he walked in with four guys that were part of his security, and they immediately came to my room. Everyone was in all black, with Elijah's dreads wildly everywhere, walking with that wide strut of his. When he saw my face, his mouth dropped.

"Damn," one of the guys said as I tried looking away.

"Shit, they got yo' ass good, baby," Elijah let out, coming over to me as he got a closer look, touching my swollen jaw. "Yo, get her shit and put it in the truck. We gotta catch this next flight back out to L.A.," he demanded. While he helped me get dressed, the guys were in and out of the apartment, with my things bagged and boxed up, clearing any trace of me living there in the first place.

The door opened to Jade's room, and she stood in the doorway, arms folded across her chest, watching. Nobody said a word. Elijah looked at her, almost as if he contemplated saying something, before dropping his head with a slow shake.

"Where yo' boyfriend at?" he asked in a calm manner, which I was starting to learn was the first sign to his Dr. Jekyll/Mr. Hyde anger issue.

"He's yo' brother, dumbass. You should know before me, nigga," Jade popped.

Elijah glanced back at me with that, "Did this bitch just call me dumb?" look. I shook my head. Whatever he was thinking, I didn't want him to do it to her, and he understood that. Jade had a mouth on her that Trent could barely even handle, but Elijah could shut it down in seconds if he wanted to.

"Son, you got something to say, say it to me. Don't look at yo' bit—."

Without warning, Elijah grabbed her hard, making her scream, and pushed her up against the door. "That New York shit does nothing for me, ma!" he mocked, nearly spitting it out to her face as she flinched. "You used to fucking with the weakest Carter, so I understand you approach me with the same bullshit you feed my brother. But know that my name is Elijah Jodie mothafucking Carter!" he snapped for dramatic effect, making her jump as he pressed her hard up against the door, arm locked down on her neck. His dreads were wild, sweats sagging low, coming to his ankle with his Jordans on.

"Let's go, Jordyn." I followed him without so much as a glance in her direction as he walked out, door closing shut behind us.

Elijah hadn't even told me I was flying to L.A. with him, and at this point, I didn't care that I was missing class, that my phone was dead, or that I didn't have an extra change of clothes. I looked a fucking wreck in the face and felt worse, but the moment I sat in first class with him on the plane, I was at peace. He looked down at me in the seat next to mine, smirking. It was a comfortable silence in first class, with food being served and drinks being poured. It was nice. Fancy. First time I ever rode first class.

"Yo, you gotta learn how to fight, baby," he said with a small laugh. I rolled my eyes in annoyance. Clearly, that was obvious. "I mean, they fucked yo' shit up bad, but you still look good, though."

"Shut up, Elijah," I mumbled, and he laughed.

"Aye, I ever tell you the story of how I got fucked up by some big nigga down the block from my house? I was like fifteen when this shit happened. Nigga kept fucking with Trent, so I went up, and was like, bruh, wassup?" he let out, acting out the story as I watched him, fist in the air. "Back then, I was skinny as shit, and this nigga had me beat by like a fucking whale baby. I mean, bruh-man was big as shit. But you know me. I ain't scared of nobody or nothing, so Trent and I take this nigga on, and bop!" he let out, fist jamming the air. "Nigga caught me in the jaw before just going the fuck in on both of us. Maaan . . . when I tell you I went back home crying to my brother Shy like a bitch? I was pissed off because I lost. I got a lot of mouth, so you know I gotta be able to back that shit up."

"So what did Shy do?" I asked softly. I watched him smile as he thought back.

"Shiloh beat my ass on the spot for coming to him crying in the first place," he said with a small laugh. "So, not only did I just get my shit fucked up by ol' boy, but I come home to my big brother, and he slams me down too, going the fuck in on my face. He didn't touch Trent, but Trent didn't cry like I did. He told me, don't ever cry after losing a fucking fight. You get the fuck up, and hold yo' head up, li'l nigga. Strength, courage, and all that other bullshit he was preaching at the time. I'm like, but this nigga calling Trent gay and shit! Shiloh kept it calm, though. Told me, I win some and I lose some. Learn from my mistakes and keep it moving. I learned that talking the loudest don't mean you the baddest. You feel me?" he asked, looking at me. I nodded. "Just because you all quiet, they intimidated by you, baby. Then they saw what you was looking like at the party that night too? You got them hoes scared as fuck, baby," he said as I closed my eyes, thinking.

"So, was that the last fight you ever lost?"

"Nah, I lost one more after that, and then I haven't lost since. That's by myself, but if Trent is with me, then ain't no point in fighting us really," he said, shrugging as he took a sip of his drink. I looked up at him, tattoos piercing hard against his dark complexion, and he smirked at me.

"What happened to the big guy? Did Shy ever go fight him?"

"On some real shit?" He laughed. "We haven't seen that nigga since. I know Shy got something to do with it, but nigga turned up missing. No body, no nothing. The day Shy told me he was going to take care of it was the day the nigga stopped showing up to school. So, I don't know where he's at, if he's even alive."

"What?" I gasped before wincing in pain.

Elijah just shrugged with a small laugh, looking at me. "That's what happens when you fuck with them Carter Boys, baby."

Looking at him, I thought about everything that had happened between us from the first time we had sex, how we met, till now. Watching him now as he quietly sang to himself, checking his phone, I smiled. His locs were pulled back, face was hard, yet his personality was so inviting, so addicting. Sometimes I felt like I was talking to my best friend.

"Elijah?" I started, leaning back on the seat as I looked up at him.

Fuck it. Jordyn. No man has ever scared you before, and no man ever will. I'm just going to come out and say it. If he accepts it, then that's great. If not? At least I know where we stand.

I was no longer afraid to admit that I had fallen for this man. Yeah, I said it. I was in love with him. Ugh, still don't like saying that word, but there was no other way to describe that feeling.

"Wassup?" he said, putting his phone down as he looked at me, those heavy-set eyes resting softly on my swollen face. He still looked at me like I was the most amazing thing to ever happen to him. At least, that's how I felt.

"I, um," I started, looking at my hands nervously. "I just wanted to say thank you."

He just looked at me, eyes squinting in a curious manner.

"Something else is on your mind," he stated knowingly. "I know you better than I know myself, baby. I told you about holding that shit. Speak what's on your mind. Let a nigga know what's really good."

I looked up at him, swollen eyes and all, and let out a sigh.

"I think—no," I said, shaking my head, "I know I'm in love with you. And . . ." I watched his eyes grow wide as my heart started to beat insanely fast. "I know we always joke around about being serious with each other, and I know your career doesn't call for a serious relationship with one woman. Although possible, I know it will be difficult because . . ." I had to stop before I started to ramble on about nothing having to do with how I felt. The nerdy side of me comes out when I get nervous, apparently. "I really am in love with you, and I hope you feel the same way too. I really never felt this way about any guy before and never thought I would, but . . . I want to really be with you, and hopefully be the only girl in your life," I mumbled off, barely able to look at him.

He was speechless. It felt like the whole plane fell silent waiting on his answer as he dropped his head with a slow shake.

"Jordyn, why you trying to do a nigga like this right now?" He groaned, slowly dragging a hand over his face as my heart literally felt like it was stuck in my throat. "You know I got love for you, but . . . I don't know. I'm not really ready to be—"

I just put my hand up, nodding my head, already knowing the answer. "It's cool," I said with a small, weak smile.

"Nah, listen. You know out of any girl I fuck with, you are my main. You are my priority before any other bitch," he continued, grabbing my hand as if he was making it better. "I just . . . that love shit isn't really how I'm feeling about you, and I like what we got going on now. When we together, we together; when we're not, we're not."

"Yeah, yeah." I nodded, feeling the pressure to hold back tears of rejection. I'd experienced rejection, but this was something different. Something I wasn't prepared for. In the midst of it, I could feel myself hardening up that exterior, my heart, and my emotions.

"Aye, look at me," Elijah said, smiling as he took my chin, making me look directly at him. "We good? I mean, I don't want shit to change between us. If you need space from me, if you think that's going to help, just let me know. I told you girls be falling for a nigga like it's nothing," he teased as I put on a fake smile, throwing a fake chuckle his way.

"It's cool, Elijah," was all I said, looking him directly in the eye.

"You sure, baby?" he pressed. I nodded. "A'ight then, come on now, Jordyn with a Y, don't slip up and fall for yo' boy. Fucking up a good thing, baby," he teased, and I smiled, watching him get back on his phone, no doubt texting another girl.

Never will I put myself through this again with him.

IHOP

Noelle

"So how was the lunch date?" Layla asked over the phone as I munched down on a fruit salad I'd made earlier. I tucked my feet underneath me as I sat on the couch in my newly furnished living room. Thank goodness Daddy came through for me, buying all of my furniture, all warm colors, just delivered this afternoon. Eventually we were going to decorate my entire place. Right now, the basic cream-colored sofa and love seat were all I needed, with a glass coffee table. I had a rug and a TV up against the wall, but no cable. Probably not for a while anyway.

"Uh, hellooo," Layla cooed as I tuned back into the conversation. "So, you just gonna go silent on me when I mention Shiloh?"

"The date was fine." I shrugged with a small smile to myself. "He really doesn't talk much, so it's hard to tell what he's thinking or how he feels about me."

"Girl!" She laughed. "That nigga was staring at you so hard at that club the other night, I can't believe you didn't feel that shit. He could have burned a hole right through you. If I was you, I would see what that stroke game is like. He looks like he know how to put it down."

"Layla, come on." I laughed, almost feeling uncomfortable at the thought. "He'll probably just stare at me the entire time."

"Shit, you might be right," she said, and we both laughed. "When are you going to see him next time?"

"Well," I said, looking at the front door, "he's supposed to be coming over tonight—"

"Whaaaaat!" she shrieked, and I closed my eyes tight at the loudness. I knew she was going to flip when I told her. "It's like that?"

"I mean, he's persistent," I said with a smile, thinking about how I was the one who had invited him over for movie night.

"So, what are y'all going to do?"

"Just watch a movie. Maybe I can get him to open up a little to me." I heard his car engine pull into the driveway. Loudest sound I ever heard. "I think he's here, Layla."

"Ooooh, don't give him the goods without seeing that dick first," she noted, and I laughed.

"I'll be sure to remember that. I gotta go," I told her quickly before hanging up.

I stood up, looking myself over. I wasn't wearing anything too revealing, nor was I trying to be overly sexy. I kept it simple, wearing some pink sleeping shorts and a white tank. I mean, yeah, I didn't have on a bra, but I really didn't like to wear those around the house anyway. My hair was up in a ponytail, bouncing about, and my dark complexion had a shine to it from the oils I used. I tidied up a bit, moving things out of the way so I didn't look like a slob just as he knocked on the door.

"Who is it?" I asked.

Silence.

I rolled my eyes as I went to the door, seeing him standing there with a bag of food in his hand. He wore a long-sleeve plaid button-up shirt with his jeans and colorful Jordans to match the shirt, a simple gold chain, with his curly hair looking neat against his fresh hair line. His low-set eyes were dark as he licked his lips at me.

"What's good?" Shiloh asked in a low voice as we hugged. The man smelled like the way a man should always smell: good. It wasn't overpowering, but it was enough to stick with my nose even after the hug.

"How was your day?" I asked, taking the food as he followed me inside, immediately kicking his shoes off like I had told him earlier.

"Straight."

Silence once again. I couldn't handle this. During the lunch date, I did most of the talking, and he seemed fine with that. Not this time. I watched him sit down on the couch, eyes shifting around the place before locking with mine. Just staring at each other.

"Why do you do that?" I snapped angrily, and his eyes lit up at the tone.

"Do what?"

"You don't say anything, but you're always staring at me like . . . like . . . " I paused, thinking about the best way to describe it. "It's annoying at times."

"I like looking at you," he said softly.

"Well, stop it. I don't like when you just stare and not say a word," I demanded.

He just looked at me once more. I rolled my eyes and turned around, placing the food on the other counter as I started to grab plates. "I bet you get a lot of girls by staring at them. I think it's rude, if you ask me," I mumbled to myself, hearing him get up from the couch. I opened up the two white containers, seeing the shiny hot lemon pepper wings in one, BBQ in another, and a whole thing of fries. Oh, hell yeah. I smiled greedily as I started to place some of everything on both plates.

"Shit," he mumbled, looking at his phone. "Aye, we may have to cut this short. I gotta go do something for my brother Ant. I forgot I promised him I would do it a while back."

"That's fine." I shrugged, taking a fry as I looked at him, wondering if I could keep the food.

"Unless you want to ride with me?" he suggested.

I froze in mid-chew, looking at him, realizing he was serious. "I guess I can go," I replied. I could have sworn I saw a smile, but maybe it was just wishful thinking. "Let me get dressed real quick."

Rushing out of the kitchen, I went to my room, digging through my boxed clothes. I needed an outfit that could blend in with whatever. Nothing too cute, but something to show off my curves. Ugh. Listen to me, trying to show off for a man that barely spoke a word to me. I threw on some cute dark blue skinny jeans and a fitted purple Nike hoodie. Luckily, the only pair of Jordans I owned had purple in them, so I brought those out and decided to wear them for the first time. I smoothed out my hair around the edges as I walked out, seeing he was on his phone.

"Yeah, I'm on the way now. Where am I supposed to drop them off at?" Shiloh said into the phone as he followed me to the front door. "A'ight, yeah, I got it. I'll be over in about fifteen minutes to get them. Make sure they ready."

"What are you getting?" I asked curiously, locking the door behind me before following him to the black Mustang. When he said nothing, I rolled my eyes. Why did I even bother with this man?

Getting in the car, I expected the smell to reek of weed, but shockingly, it smelled fresh. Like, pine fresh. As he cut the car on, I looked around the black interior, seeing his phone hooked up to the radio.

"What kind of music you like, Noelle?" he asked calmly, and I looked at him, surprised he even said my name.

"If you have any Tupac, that would be cool to listen to," I replied, and he smirked to himself, going through his playlist.

"What you know about Pac, shawty?"

"I know more than you would think, nigga," I retorted sarcastically.

"Yeah, okay." He laughed outright, backing out. The playlist started to play throughout the car as we silently jammed to Tupac, heads bobbing to the music with an occasional lyric recitation.

I watched him drive like he was cruising on a Sunday afternoon, one hand on the wheel, the other on his chin like he was in deep thought. There was no road rage, not even a hint of irritation when he drove. He looked out the window for a split second, placing that tongue on his lower lip as he turned down a street.

"Look at this nigga right here," he mumbled, rolling my window down as he pulled alongside the sidewalk, seeing a guy walking with his arm around a girl. She was barely dressed for the weather, wearing leggings, sandals, and a hoodie, while the guy sagged his jeans so low you could see it all.

"Aye, li'l nigga!" Shiloh called out as he looked back before smiling.

"Bruh! What's good!" The boy laughed as he leaned in my window, eyes immediately going over my body. "Fuck you doing here?"

"Heading over to Ant place. Nigga, pull yo' fucking jeans up when you walking with a bitch," Shiloh corrected him, and my neck snapped to him. *Bitch*?

"My bad, big homie," the boy said, pulling up his pants. "Aye, you got a rubber on you? I don't have shit on me or at the crib, bruh."

"How you know she even trying to fuck?" Shiloh teased as he reached in his glove compartment to pull out a wallet. I just watched in awe, seeing him give the boy money and a few packs of condoms.

"Because she is. Everybody ran through her. I'm just trying to get my fill in. You feel me, nigga?" The boy laughed as they slapped hands.

"Go do what you do, and yo' ass better be in school tomorrow. If Will call me talking about you missed school, you and me are going to have a problem," Shiloh said, getting serious.

The boy nodded before getting back with the girl, and we pulled off. I stared at him in amazement, not really knowing what to think at this point.

"He's your little brother too?" I asked.

"Something like that," he mumbled, turning down another street before pulling up to a small house on the corner. He blew the horn before getting out altogether, letting the cold air interfere with the warm heat circulating in the car. I watched the porch light pop on as the screen door opened. Out came four little kids, running up to Shiloh with their book bags in hand, screaming all at once.

"Tell that nigga when he get back in town, I'm going to see about his dumb ass!" the girl let out. "His stupid baby mama think she funny by dropping off all these damn kids at my place! I don't give—"

"Aye! I'm not trying to hear that shit!" Shiloh snapped. "Yo, get in the back seat," he told the kids, and they immediately raced to the car, clamoring to open the doors.

"I need some money, Shiloh," the girl whined as she stood there in a robe, patting down her weave.

As soon as the door opened, all four kids came rushing inside, talking at once, asking a million and one questions to me. Two of them had dark skin, one light, and another was brown. The three boys looked to be older than the one girl, who looked like she was three or four years old.

"Nigga, you stupid!" one boy yelled to his brother as they immediately started fighting, with the girl laughing at the chaos.

"Hey, hey!" I called out, turning around. "You don't need to hit each other like that, not in front of your sister."

"Who the fuck are you?" another boy asked, and my mouth dropped.

"Nigga, you gon' get in trouble if Uncle Shy hear you cursing," another said before punching him in the arm, starting the fight all over again. I couldn't believe I'd agreed to come along. When Shiloh walked back to the car, closing the door, they immediately calmed down.

"Uncle Shy," the girl called out in a sweet voice.

"What, baby girl?" I felt my heart immediately melt as I looked at him, watching him pull off onto the main street.

"I'm hungry," she whined, rubbing her eyes.

"I want Burger King!"

"Nah, get McDonald's! I want everything off the menu! I want all of it!"

"I don't care what I get, as long as I'm eating," the quietest boy said.

"Yo' punk ass lost earlier. You shouldn't be allowed to eat," another brother said.

Without warning, Shiloh reached behind him, grabbing the boy with the potty mouth by the head and smacking him hard, causing the rest to laugh. That whole drive was nothing but chaos, crying from the girl, and arguing from the boys, yet the moment we stopped at an IHOP and grabbed a table to sit down, the energy level slowly started to come down.

The little girl's name was Diamond, but everyone called her Baby Girl, even her brothers. The three boys were Damien, Quinton, and Sean. Baby Girl warmed up to me fast as we sat together in the booth, talking about hair and whatever else four-year-olds like to talk about. Lucky for me, I still watched cartoons in my spare time, so I knew about most of the shows she was talking about. She was adorable with beads in her braids, wearing the cutest Polo dress and matching coat with tights. Whoever the mama was, she made sure she looked cute. The boys were just as fresh.

When the food came, I helped her cut up her pancakes, while the boys tore through their food like machines. When all was said and done, Baby Girl was standing up, braiding my hair, while the boys all talked amongst themselves, playing some imaginary game.

Shiloh looked at me, smirking.

"What's funny?" I asked, feeling the light tugs at my hair.

"Nah, I just didn't imagine this happening with you and me," he stated. "My bad if this isn't your ideal date."

"I had a good time," I told him, feeling Baby Girl wrap her tiny arms around my neck as if I was leaving.

"Uncle Shy, can we do this again?" she asked in her soft voice.

"Whatever you want, baby," he told her, pulling out his wallet. He was definitely going to be the kind of man to spoil his daughter when he had kids. I could already see she had him wrapped around her finger, and she probably knew it, too, even at her age. I felt her press her mouth against my ear like she was ready to tell me a secret.

"Do you like Uncle Shy?" she asked, and I looked at her, eyes wide, before laughing.

"What she say?" he pressed curiously.

I just looked at her, nodding my head excitedly as her eyes lit up.

"You want to be his girlfriend?" she whispered loudly against my ear.

I knew Shiloh heard her this time, because his eyes squinted, looking hard at his niece.

"What you know about boyfriend and girlfriend?" he asked as I laughed.

"Let her be. She's asking me the questions, not you," I teased as I looked at her, nodding my head.

"Ahh!" She freaked excitedly before getting down, only to get on the seat next to Shiloh to whisper in his ear, tiny hands trying to cover up her mouth.

"Yeah." Shiloh smiled.

"So, you boyfriend and girlfriend now," she stated proudly, hand on top of her Uncle's head. "You gotta kiss her, Uncle!"

"Right now?"

"Oh my God." I laughed, feeling so embarrassed. Even the boys stopped doing what they were doing to watch in excitement.

"Yeah, you gotta kiss her!" Quinton chimed in.

"On the mouth!" Baby Girl pressed as I felt my face burn, feeling flushed. This could not be happening right now, four kids trying to set me and Shiloh up in a relationship on the spot.

"If I kiss her in front of y'all, I don't want to hear nothing about it—"

"Kiss her!" they all let out as I laughed. He shook his head before getting up to come to my side of the table.

"What are you doing, Shiloh?" I asked, feeling my heartbeat. It felt like everyone in the restaurant was watching this, wanting to see the kiss. Even the waitresses stopped, wanting to see the exchange. He licked his lips as he gently cupped my chin, hovering just above my lips as I closed my eyes.

"Kiss her! Uncle, do it!" Baby Girl shrieked in excitement as I heard the people in the restaurant cheer him on. I opened my eyes, seeing him staring at me, fingers still cupping my chin.

"You gonna be mine?" he asked in such a low voice that only I could hear it.

"Yeah," I replied.

He smiled before placing those lips on mine. I heard everyone clap while the kids freaked out in disgust.

"Ewwwww!" the boys let out in a gross manner.

He pulled back, looking at his nephews with a smile. "Y'all li'l niggas too young to get it now. Wait until you get older. You'll be kissing on any girl you get yo' hands on," he said. They immediately showed their protest and disgust at that statement as we both laughed.

Love Much

Tyree

"Bitch, I don't know," I said with a sigh as I applied makeup on one of my clients. I was at a photo shoot in Midtown for a vixen magazine. Hip hop was big in Atlanta. Shit, black people doing ratchet shit for money was big in Atlanta, so best believe a nigga was finna get in on that cash. Not only do I style ya, but I will have that face beat and hair looking right. I can do it all. So, it was a Wednesday afternoon, and I was working on my client and best friend, Harlem, for her photo shoot. She was one of the top exotic dancers in Atlanta, the most sought-after bad bitch, with her hazel eyes pulling niggas left and right if she wanted to.

"Well, has he tried making it up to you?" Harlem pressed, asking about Ontrell fuck-ass Carter. "You can't not speak to him just because you see a few text messages in his phone last night. You need to address that shit."

"For what?" I snapped, looking at her before continuing on her eye makeup. "This nigga has been cheating on me probably since day one."

"If that's the case, why haven't you left him?"

I sighed, thinking about the only answer that I could ever give. "Because I still love him, and I hope one day he will change," I mumbled, flipping her hair off her shoulders. "You know I love that man."

"And I know he loves you, but sometimes you need to step away for a minute for him to realize that. He might be the type of nigga that doesn't know what he has until it's gone."

"I'm not ready to be gone. I don't even know what the fucking single life is like anymore. I don't want to date again or go through bum-ass niggas just to make myself feel better for even going out. I'm not trying to do that. I like coming home to a clean house, with my man cooking or waiting up for me, or vice versa."

"I know that's right," Harlem agreed just as they called for her name.

As soon as she walked onto the set, I sat down on the chair, going through my phone. Ontrell was out of town this week, doing performances with his brothers. Ugh. As much as this nigga pissed me off on a daily basis, I felt like I almost worshipped the ground he walked on. I wasn't going to find another man like him, so secure in his sexuality and yet masculine to a T. Except when it came to me. I brought the bitch out of him a couple of times. He was attractive, pulling bitches and niggas on the same day, but I know I deserved better. I just didn't know if I could get better.

I looked down at my fit for the day, wearing gray jeans, thick calf-high socks with my riding boots, cute black long-sleeve top, light gray and black scarf around my neck, and a black skull cap. Since I had no hair, a nigga had to keep her scalp covered during this weather. I was cute. I stayed looking good and smelled like Yves Saint Laurent's finest cologne.

Looking back at my phone as I crossed my legs, I started going through pictures of Trell and me—the countless selfies we took together in the bed, on date nights that we used to go on, pictures we sent to each other while we were apart. *SMH. Two years.* If this man asked me to marry him tomorrow, I would be at that chapel with bells on. Yet, the pain and hurt he put me through always ran in the back of my mind. Looking at the picture he sent me of him laying in the bed with a sad face with the caption, IT'S WEIRD SLEEPING WITHOUT YOU FOR THIS LONG, I smiled. I loved looking at my chocolate boo, locs sprawled out on the pillow, with those almond-shaped eyes and thick lips. *Damn, Trell, why do you have to be the way you are?* He was the love of my life. He was the man I was meant to be with. I just didn't think he realized it yet.

Going through more pictures, I suddenly felt a presence behind me. Before I could turn around, I heard the voice.

"I see you can't call nobody, but you can look at a nigga's picture," the voice said as my mouth dropped. I was afraid to turn around and look.

No, while y'all reading this thinking it was some romantic-ass shit, hoping it was Ontrell, guess again. I looked back, seeing my on- and off-again ex, Eric, standing behind me with his coat on, looking . . . damn. He was my height, with light skin, a trimmed beard, and a muscular body he kept in shape. He almost puts you in the mind of Common, but thicker.

I got up, smiling as I reached out for a quick hug and felt my body respond to his. Damn, it had been a minute. Before Ontrell, there was Eric, my older nigga. He caught me fresh out of high school, being six years older than me. Our relationship was . . . stressful. It was wild, exciting, trying, violent, and romantic all in one. His problem was a control issue. When he didn't get his way, he became violent. Oddly enough, as I was ending things with him, that's when I was introduced to Ontrell. He knew my situation from the get-go and instantly showed me something better, showed me loved like I'd never experienced before.

"How are you, boo?" I asked, sitting back down in the chair with my legs crossed as he stood in front of me, smiling while looking me over. "Nah-uh, nigga, you know I got a man, so don't even try it."

"You don't even know why I came by." He laughed, pulling up a chair. "I just moved back to Atlanta for a business opportunity and thought I'd hit you up. Didn't even realize you changed your number on me."

"I did," I stated, taking a sip of my water.

"So, how you been, Tyree? I missed you," he let out.

I took a deep swallow, feeling myself start to sweat. Nigga still had an effect on me for some reason.

"I've been doing good. You know . . . working, trying to make money."

"You still with ol' boy, the young nigga?"

"He's a year younger, so chill," I snapped.

"I'm saying, you go from a man to a boy." He laughed, hand on his chest.

"What the fuck do you want, Eric?" I pressed, clearly annoyed.

He licked his lips as he pulled his phone out, handing it to me. "I just want to catch up. I grew up a lot since we last spoke, and I know it was a lot of things I did that was fucked up. So, I just want to clear the air. Nothing more, boo."

"Not yo' boo, so correct yo' self, nigga," I snapped, and he laughed.

"I'm sorry, Tyree. Just please, let me get your number. I can take you out somewhere nice to eat, and let me just say what I have to say. You don't have to speak to me, call me up, none of that ever again."

I stared at the phone before deciding to just go ahead and give him my number. No harm in that. I could hear what the nigga had to say, plus it had been a minute since I went out to eat with another man. Eric was definitely on that grown shit, something I rarely experienced with Ontrell these days.

So, of course, you know when I got home, I immediately called up my girls to tell them what had happened, gossiping like I was about that life while making something to eat. Wasn't shit in the house to eat since I hadn't been grocery shopping that week, so I just heated up a pack of noodles, lounging around in my boxer briefs and long socks.

"So, are you going to see him?" Niya asked. "I still think you can do better than both of these niggas, but maybe Eric is the exact nigga to keep Ontrell on his feet."

"Girl," I said, smacking my teeth with a roll of my eyes. "Ontrell and jealousy don't mix. Trust me, let him even hear me talk about another nigga on TV and he pops the fuck off. I can't mention another nigga, but he can fuck the world and expect me to be okay with it."

"I'm sure, because he's used to you staying put and not stepping outside of the relationship. Can you imagine if you told this nigga you had a date with yo' ex-boyfriend, let alone fucking the nigga?"

"Oh God!" I laughed, thinking about the reaction. Ontrell would probably shit on himself if he ever knew. "Anyway, I don't know what I'm going to do about—" I stopped in mid-sentence, hearing the front door being unlocked. "Hold up, Niya." I got up from the couch and looked down the hallway, seeing Trell walk in with a bunch of roses and multiple bags, struggling to carry it all.

I immediately hung up as I walked over to him. "Why are you back so early?" I asked, confused, as he looked at me with wide eyes.

"Nigga, how about fucking helping me? This is yo' shit," he snapped, and I immediately grabbed the roses and bags, taking it to the living room. I couldn't help myself. I was cheesing so hard like a kid on Christmas. I could even smell the food he had got from Maggianos. He knew that was my favorite spot to eat.

Walking back to the door, I watched him bring in his suitcases and more shopping bags from some of my favorite stores in New York. As soon as he closed the door, I leaned up against the wall, looking at him. He looked like he had just woken up from a long plane ride. He wore bandana print harem pants with a hoodie, locs pulled back, with his gray Jordans. He smiled at me with his pearly whites against his dark brown complexion, thinking he was cute.

"Nah, nigga, you already know you ain't shit to me right now," I snapped, and his smiled dropped.

"Come on, Tyree. I came back home early, got you all this shit, and you still want to start something?" he complained as he walked over to me, eyeing my bare chest in pure lust. I put my hand up to stop him, but he wrapped his arms around me, hugging me tight as I laughed.

"Trell, I'm being serious," I let out as he play-fully attacked my neck, biting it before kissing it. "Nigga, you know you fucked up with me."

"I know, and I'm sorry," he said against me. "Come on. You standing here looking like you trying to get some, but you won't even let me hug you? Yo' own nigga can't even hug you now?" he pressed as he let go, looking at me like he was shocked, trying to play victim.

I rolled my eyes. *This nigga here, I swear.*

"What did you get me, Trell?" I asked instead, and he smiled.

We immediately started to chow down on our food from Maggianos, going through each shopping bag as he showed me what he got. I don't think I'd ever been happier, realizing my own boyfriend knew my exact style of dress, my sense of fashion, and the stores that I liked shopping at. It was a small proud moment in the relationship for me, almost making me forget about Eric.

So, he was sitting on the couch, already in basketball shorts and socks with no shirt on, eating, while I sat on the end, with my feet propped up in his lap. Clothes and shoes were all over the living room floor, with the roses sitting in a pretty vase on the coffee table. It felt good to have him home for once, and not us arguing all the damn time.

"Baby, guess who came up to the shoot today," I started, taking a bite of the pasta.

He looked at me, mouth full of food, eating like a little boy with no manners. "Who?"

"Eric," I let out.

His chewing slowly came to a stop as he stared hard at me.

"He just showed up there, talking about he moved to Atlanta and wanted to take me out to eat to apologize. And you know what? I think I'm going to take him up on that," I stated.

Trell's head cocked back, eyes wide.

Yeah, nigga, I said it, and I'm telling you.

"Oh, so you just think I'm going to let you walk out with yo' ex-nigga on a date and think I'm going to be cool with that shit?" Trell let out angrily. "Why the fuck does he know where you fucking work at in the first place?"

"Why does it matter? It's a free meal, and I get an apology for all the shit he put me through. Uh, nigga? I'm going," I stated, and he shook his head, continuing to eat.

"We'll see," was all he said, then we ate in tense silence.

I finished up my plate, grabbing his as he continued to look through the outfits, putting stuff together and taking pictures of it. He was upset, but nigga, I was upset every time I was around him. Every time he did some stupid-ass shit, I was upset, so at this point, I couldn't care less about his mood.

"I'm going to bed," I told him, walking to the back room. I'd bought brand new bed sheets yesterday, and a nice wine-colored bedspread for the queen-size bed. I'd already taken my shower, so now I was just relaxing in my plush bed, feeling the cool sheets against my skin when he walked in, closing the door behind him. I ignored him as he went into the bathroom, taking his shower while I popped the TV on. I knew his thing was sports, so I had it on ESPN while I went through my personal lookbook for this season, putting together looks for different clients, on my phone, searching for inspiration. Work didn't stop for anyone. I always tried to either have the best, or imitate the best. Some of my clients were on budgets but wanted to look like they didn't have to worry about money, while others were about that money life. So, I was constantly doing online shopping, buying shoes, bundles of hair, and makeup items.

When he walked out fully naked, I couldn't help but look, seeing he was on hard. Nigga was trying me tonight. I could tell. He already knew how to get me going, I just wasn't going to fall into it.

I continued to focus on my work as he slipped into the bed beside me, resting his head on my side, looking at the TV.

"You want to go to the game with me Sunday?" he asked, talking about the Falcons game. He knew I wasn't into sports, but I nodded.

"Did you already buy the tickets?" I asked, looking down at my man, the love of my life, as he rest his head against me.

"Nah, I'll get 'em in the morning. I want some good-ass seats, too," he said. When he saw that I was scrolling through my fashion blog on my phone, he asked, "You ordered my shit for next week? I've been eyeing them shoes for a month now."

"I just got the tracking number for them, baby," I said softly, handing him the phone as I continued to go through my notebook, looking at the different looks I'd put together in the past. Pictures of my clients, pictures of dresses, heels—everything was all in this notebook. I had a total of three notebooks with the exact same thing too.

See! This is what the fuck I was talking about: laying in the bed with your man, enjoying each other's company. I could tell he was irritated with me, but he had a bad habit of sleeping up under me. When he said it was hard to sleep without me in the same bed as him, he wasn't lying. I'd woken up to him completely draped over me, arms, legs, everything. Another time,

I almost rolled over this nigga, not realizing he slept right up under me like a damn child. I used to cuss him out about that shit, but now I couldn't help but find it cute.

He looked up at me and our eyes locked.

"What, nigga?" he pressed, and I smiled. My thug-ass man always approached me like that. He never made me feel inferior, or like a bitch. He recognized that I was a man and wanted to keep it that way. It was another reason why I didn't think I would find another one like him.

"I love you, Ontrell Carter," I told him softly, seeing him smile.

"I love you too, Tyree Carter," he stated, poking his lips out for a kiss.

I loved it when he gave me his last name. I bent down as he came up, with our lips locking.

"I'd love you even more if you didn't fuck with that nigga."

"I won't. I just said it to piss you off," I admitted.

His eyes cut low as his lips pursed like, *Nigga, I knew it*.

I just cheesed with a small, helpless shrug, watching him sit up so he could lay on top of me, putting my book aside.

"You ain't shit, nigga," he said as I laughed, arms coming around his neck. I definitely wasn't ready to let him go. Didn't think I would ever be.

***

Guess I spoke too soon. As usual, I woke up in the middle of the night, wanting something to drink. Glancing at the clock on the dresser, I saw that it was going on three. I looked down, seeing Ontrell holding on to my body like it was the last night he would ever see me. So, careful not to wake him, I gently slid out of the bed, body sore from the wonderful sex with my future husband.

Walking out of the room, my body was completely nude as I went to the kitchen. I saw where his phone was vibrating on the counter, and you know a nigga couldn't help himself. I grabbed it, seeing a number I didn't recognize.

"Hello?" I answered, putting on my nigga voice, trying to sound like Trell.

"Baby, where are you?" a guy asked as my heart started to pound.

A nigga this time, Ontrell? Like, really? My dick wasn't good enough?

"I miss you. Even though you came by last night, I still miss you."

"Last night?" I repeated, regular voice. "Who the fuck is this?"

"Uh, who the fuck is this? This better not be no other nigga answering my man's phone like they together," the man snapped.

"Son, it's another nigga answering my man's phone!" I popped, feeling my Northern accent come out heavy. "Who the fuck is this? You stay in Atlanta?"

"Damn right I do. Trell and me been fucking for a year. So, who the fuck is this? What? You his little side piece?" He laughed. "Huh? Him and I are engaged to be married next year. Got the rings to prove it."

"You what?" I shrieked, looking at the number. "Nigga, get off my man's phone, playing these little-ass games like you are. I've been with him for two years. I know his family, all his brothers, and we live together. He's sleeping in our bed as we speak. So, while you been riding the booty call train night after night, know that this nigga will always come home to me, son. Know this!" I hung up, nearly throwing the phone hard against the wall, feeling disgusting all over again for even sleeping with him. He'd been in Atlanta this whole time. I can't . . .

Me yelling was going to do nothing but start the cycle all over again. Instead? I was going to get even. I grabbed my phone after getting my drink and texted Eric, telling him I could meet with him whenever he was free.

Tia

"Girl, it is too packed out here!" Porscha yelled as she, and my other friend Niya and I walked, arms linked together, to the back woods behind the school, where they were throwing a block party. It was Homecoming Week festivities. I wasn't going to be a pregnant bum about it. I did still want to participate. Thursday night, no classes until Monday? Shit, I was down. I had gone to the hospital earlier that week, and they confirmed what I already knew. I couldn't pronounce the shit, but I did have a severe case of morning sickness. They told me I was dehydrated and needed to eat only . . . shit I don't remember. I knew I had to start taking better care of myself since my body was going through all these changes.

I hadn't spoken to Jahiem since, only to tell him I went to the doctor's and to explain to him what was wrong. That was Monday. I hadn't heard from the nigga since. That was the same day I decided to beat that bitch Jordyn's ass. We're not going to even get into that, though. Not my story to tell. I'm sure you read her shit, and she said what it was. I'm not going back. It happened, and best believe if given the opportunity, I would do it again. Period. Never liked her lame ass in the first place.

"Bitch, look at this shit," Niya said as we looked around, seeing it was so packed out here in these streets in the middle of the night. People had booths set up, tents set up where they were cooking food, the roads were shut down so people could walk the streets freely, and I mean, everybody and their mama was out here. This was only the first night. Shit was going to happen every night until Sunday.

So, you know we were all looking fly as always. I wasn't going to let a baby growing in me stop a bitch from turning up, okay? I had a fresh weave in, all black with blonde tips. I had on cute leggings, with a cute semi-cropped hoodie and Jordans. Booty was sitting right, hips poked out; I was pulling niggas' attention without even realizing it. Weave was straight, falling down my back with a side swoop, decked out in the finest accessories. I looked cute. Fuck you think? All of us looked cute.

"Girl, these niggas out here looking good as hell," Porscha said as we all eyed two guys walking past us, heads turning to check each other out.

"What up?" one called out as we turned back around, laughing.

"Nigga is a little boy. I need a grown man," Niya retorted.

"I know that's right." I smirked, eyes scanning the heads on the street, looking for any familiar face or cute nigga I could snatch up. Even with my pregnant ass, I was always looking.

"You haven't talked to yo' baby daddy at all?" Niya asked, and I rolled my eyes.

"Please don't ruin a bitch's mood by calling him my baby daddy," I retorted, and they laughed, thinking I was playing. "I don't want to associate myself with that lame-ass nigga. And no, I haven't spoken to him since."

"Can't be too many dudes out here that is willing to help you with a baby they don't even think is theirs. You need to give him more credit than what you do," Porscha reasoned as I looked at my best friend, eyes wide in shock.

"Bitch, I didn't want to sleep with him! Have we forgot how all of this started? He raped my ass."

"Aye, beautiful ladies," someone called out, and we turned around, seeing a group of guys behind us. I recognized a few of them from the football team. "Where y'all walking to?"

"Why you wanna know?" Porscha asked, instantly getting into flirty mode, knowing she had a man.

"I mean, shit, we trying to see what's good," one said as his eyes landed on me.

I smiled as we let our small clique mingle and mix with them, walking as one set. Music was blasting from different directions, houses on the street had their porch lights on, signaling that they were part of the fun for the night, and I felt like nothing could kill my vibe. I had a red cup in my hand, filled with water, of course, because that's all my friends were allowing me to drink. They wouldn't even let me put a splash of sugar in that bitch. We kept walking, throwing cute smiles and flirty laughs at the dudes as my eyes continued to look around. I felt good, and my mood was on point for once—until I saw that infamous red Camaro. I stopped walking and stared at the car, seeing Jahiem sitting on the hood with at least ten girls surrounding him, all looking basic as fuck.

"Watch me fuck up this nigga's night just because I can," I said, handing my drink to

Niya as I walked across the street toward him. I flipped my hair off my shoulder as I daintily wiped the edges of my lips gloss off my lips, catching his eyes real quick. He sat there thinking he was so cute with his basic-ass white shirt, black leather jacket, black jeans, and black Gucci high-top sneakers with the red stripe going down the back; yet something was off about him. I looked him over again before realizing nigga had cut his dreads off. He had clean, low-cut hair with the edges lined up, no beard, and a clean face. It made him look his age instead of thrity-something. Damn. We locked eyes as I licked my lips. Shit, that changed his features for the better. His dark brown eyes seemed sexier, and those plump, dark pink lips looked fuller, and his teeth seemed whiter.

"Jahiem, you so sexy," a girl cooed as she rubbed his head, making him smile. Nigga even had dimples.

"Thank you, baby," he said as I walked right up to the group of girls, making my way past them so I could stand in front of him, arms folded over my chest.

"Uh, bitch, you could have said excuse—"

I turned to her so quick, eyebrow raised like, *What?*

"I don't speak basic," I said, giving the ho one look before flipping my hair back as I rolled my neck back to him. "Nigga, you got some nerve to be at my school flirting with these hoes knowing I'm pregnant with yo' damn baby," I snapped, and the girls gasped. I didn't have to do it, but I wanted to fuck up his night because he'd fucked up my life.

"Hold up. We—"

"Nah-uh, don't act like that shit didn't happen!" I continued, finger pointing in his face as I put on my ghetto-bitch voice. "Nigga, how you gon' give me the best sex of my life, tell me you love me, and then leave me for the next ho?" I cried.

"Oh, nah-uh, girl. Let's go," one of the girls said as she grabbed her friend.

I smirked as his mouth dropped.

"You doing that shit on purpose! I didn't—"

"I loved you, Jahiem! How can you do this to me? To us? I'm having yo' fucking baby, nigga. The least you can do is show some respect." I flipped, mushing him in the forehead as all the girls started to back away from him in disgust.

"Bruh, you got her pregnant?" one guy asked as I backed up, smiling.

"Fuck is yo' problem, Tia?" he snapped, standing straight up and directly in front of me.

"I just wanted to fuck up yo' night, nigga, that's all." I shrugged with a hair flip and a cute smile before walking off. My friends were cracking up in the middle of street, camera phones up, recording the whole thing.

"Bitch, you so crazy!" Niya laughed. "You see his face?"

I just kept walking until I felt a hand grab my arm. I turned around to an angry Jahiem, looking like he wanted to fuck my ass up.

"That was uncalled for, Tia," he said in a low voice, still not letting go.

"Yeah, well, it happened. I just did it to get a laugh, bruh. But I know you better let go of my fucking arm before—"

"Nah, you staying by my side for the rest of the night. You want to fuck up my night, I'm going to fuck yours up by being near you. Aye!" he called out to my friends, still holding my arm as I snatched it free. "Go on. She staying with me."

"Uh, okay," Porscha and Niya let out, smiling hard to themselves. I already knew that look as I watched Porscha quickly come up to me, handing me my red cup.

"Bitch, don't even." I laughed, taking it as she smirked at the two of us before walking off.

He walked back over to the car, leaning on the hood as I stood in front of him, about to take a sip when he snatched the cup from me.

"What is this?" he asked, smelling it as I laughed at his dumb ass.

"New drink called water, nigga," I said, snatching it back. "You heard of it before?"

He smirked as he watched me drink, looking my body over while tucking in that lower lip like he was cute.

Nigga, you ain't cute. Barely. I took a few steps away from him.

"Come here," he coaxed, and I looked at him like he'd lost his mind before continuing to enjoy the music, rocking back and forth on my clean Jordans. The house we stood near was playing Gucci, and I knew just about every song that man had ever created.

"So, you just going to stand all the way over there? I can come to you if you want, but you don't want that shit to happen." He continued as I looked at him. "You look good. I was just trying to get a better look at what you got on."

"Nigga, for what?" I laughed while slowly walking toward him.

He just smiled at me, licking his lips as I stood directly in front of him. Damn, he had a nice thick-ass body to him. I was good with slim niggas, but he had some weight to him that was perfectly molded into the perfect body. I flipped my hair off my shoulder before stretching it out in a flirty way, placing it right back over my shoulder as we stared at each other.

"Fuck you want, nigga?" I barked cutely.

"I can't just look at you?" he asked with a laugh.

"Nope." I smiled, turning my attention toward the street as I started reciting the lyrics to "Freaky Girl," rapping to no one in particular. A couple of guys walked by, and one caught my eye quick as he stopped, lifting his head up at me.

"What's good, shawty?" he asked, and I immediately cringed at the word "shawty."

"Where you from?" I asked, walking toward him, leaving Jahiem's ass to sit on his little car, watching. His homeboys kept walking as he smiled sneakily at me, rubbing his hands together like he was about to try some shit.

"Shit, where you think I'm from, ma? With yo' sexy ass," he pressed, eyeing me hard. He was a dark-skin nigga with a box juice fade, thinking he was about some shit, wearing his fake gold chain and old Jordans he tried to keep clean. He was cute in the face, but everything else screamed *lame*.

"New York?" I asked, and he laughed.

"Nah, guess again, baby girl. Damn, where yo' man at? He mind if I take you for the night? Because you got to be the finest girl out here," he said, and Jahiem let out a snort.

I looked back, cutting my eyes hard at him, seeing he was trying to keep from laughing.

"You call me lame, but this nigga look like the coolest crackhead on the street, shawty? Like, real shit? This is what you into?" Jahiem asked with a laugh. "I see why you wasn't trying to fuck with me like that."

"Jahiem, don't—"

"Nah, B, fuck you trying to say, nigga?" The guy tensed up, Northern accent becoming thick as hell.

"Nigga, I just said that shit. Don't call me no fucking B. We don't talk like that down here, nigga. Get it right." Jahiem laughed, still chilling on the car like it was nothing. He was such a fucking clown, thinking everything was funny.

"Jahiem, you need to stop," I warned, hearing this guy's breathing become heavy.

Without warning, he placed his hand on me, pushing me to the side, almost making me fall on my damn self. Damn sho' made me drop my cup of water.

"Nigga, you almost—"

He stepped up to Jahiem, who immediately changed gears as he got off the car, lifting his shirt to reveal the gun he kept tucked inside.

"Bruh, try that shit!" Jahiem warned as he stepped closer to the guy, who started backing up. "Nigga, you come for her, you getting me, bruh, so fuck with me if you want to, my nigga," he snapped, still exposing his gun.

I was still heated, so I wasn't even done going off on this lame nigga. I regained my posture and stepped to him too, with Jahiem directly behind me as backup.

"Nigga, don't ever put yo' hands on me!" I snapped, hand all in his face as he continued to back up.

"Fuck you!" He spat instead. "Ugly bitch-ass—"

"Who you calling ugly?" I retorted, looking myself over. I looked back at Jahiem while pointing at myself. "Nigga, I'm ugly? Shit, I thought I was cute."

"Nah, you fine as fuck, baby. He know it too," Jahiem answered, eyes hard on the guy. "You wish you had a bitch as fine as mine, nigga. Fuck on before I put a hole in yo' chest."

"Whatever, fuck-ass nigga," the guy mumbled as he damn near took off running to reach his friends again.

"Shit, got me fucked up," I mumbled, finger-combing my hair as I turned back to look at Jahiem, who chilled back on the hood of his car like it was nothing. "And why the fuck you walking around with that?"

"Because niggas get stupid out here," he retorted.

I rolled my eyes. "I still hate that he made me drop my water," I mumbled as I looked at the red cup on the curb.

"Stay put. I'll get you another one. I need a drink my damn self," Jahiem said as he hopped off the car and walked in the middle of the street, looking for whoever was selling alcoholic beverages and water at the same time. Damn, I was still mad at that. Couldn't wait to tell my friends about that shit.

Walking over to the red Camaro, I sat on top of the hood, propping my feet up as I watched Jahiem walk back, looking like a model with that leather jacket on. Maybe it was the haircut, or the way he defended me, but I was starting to find him attractive.

He stepped up to the curb, giving a heads up to someone from afar as he handed me a bottle of water.

"Why you don't have no girlfriend?" I asked curiously.

"Because of my job. No girl can handle the constant traveling, the partying, the late nights, none of that shit. I tried it already, and either she end up breaking up with me, or I end up fucking around," he said, shrugging. "Now I got a baby on the way, so you really think I'm about to be pulling bitches?"

"You sound mad about it," I mumbled sarcastically with an eye roll.

He took a sip of his cup, eyes never leaving mine. "Nah, I've accepted the fact that you really keeping this baby, and there is nothing I can do to change yo' mind just because I'm not ready to be a fucking dad. Not with the lifestyle I got."

"Well, I'm not ready to be a mom either, but I'll get ready for when the day comes. You still have the option to bounce, nigga. I told you I don't need you," I snapped with a hair flip.

He said nothing, just stood there bobbing his head to the music as more people walked by.

"I'm serious, Jahiem. I really don't need you like that."

"Nah, but that baby is going to need me," was all he said, and I felt my heart melt. Damn, that was a man right there.

We chilled in silence as I hopped down from the car, seeing the streets become more crowded

as more people started to show up. The moment
the song switched to Gucci's "Trap House," I was
lit.

"Aye! This is my shit!" I yelled out with a hand
in the air.

Jahiem just looked at me with a laugh. "What
yo' ol' college-educated ass know about this
song?" he asked.

"Nigga, I'm the biggest Gucci fan you will
ever meet," I said, flipping my hair back as I
recited word for word the lyrics to the song, all
in Jahiem's face as he laughed.

"Maaan, you better sit down somewhere,
talking about trap house. You don't know nothing about the trap house," he cracked as I turned
around on him, hand still in the air as I backed
up on him, singing the song. "Aye, aye, calm
down with yo' wannabe thug ass. Fuck is you
doing?" He laughed as I continued to wild out on
him, pressing that booty on him like he knew he
wanted it. He slipped an arm around my waist to
keep me still just as a couple of guys walked up,
greeting him.

"Bruh, what's good?" one said as they slapped
hands. Jahiem immediately went back to
holding on to me as he started talking to the
guys. I'm not going to even lie; I was definitely
comfortable being held by him. The touch was
so familiar; it almost felt like he belonged.

"Nah, I was telling that bitch the other day to leave. She went crazy on me," one guy said with a shake of his head. "Slashed my tires, broke my windows. I mean, she went the fuck off on my car. I'm like, we was only fucking, it wasn't nothing more than that."

"You can't just keep having sex with a girl thinking she's not going to catch feelings," I chimed in.

"Even if you tell her what it is from the get-go?" another asked.

"It doesn't matter. You knew that shit was going to happen. No female can have sex without feelings if you steady fucking her," I stated.

"I fucked with plenty of girls that never caught feelings," he argued, and I laughed.

"That means she was fucking somebody else then," I said, watching his face drop.

Everyone laughed, seeing he wasn't expecting that answer. Men can be so clueless and blind when they think they're the only ones. No, boo. Not always the case.

We all fell into an easy conversation about relationships before it turned to sports and parties. I was out of the loop at that point, so I just continued to drink the rest of my water, occasionally texting Porscha to see if she was still here and what she was doing afterward. I didn't even realize Jahiem was looking down at me, watching, until he brought his head down toward my ear.

"You want to spend the night with me?" he asked in a low voice.

My body went through so many different levels of chills I had to mentally calm myself down as I nodded my head. It was like an unspoken agreement or bond that was just made. Don't know what changed between the two of us, but I know I hadn't planned on going there to spend the night with my baby daddy. Shit, it had been so long that having dick wouldn't hurt me. If anything, it would calm me down. If it was anything like last time, I already knew I was in for the best sex I ever had. Just like that, Jahiem went back into the conversation, still holding on to me.

When we decided to make our leave, this nigga here was so ignorant. It was the only car on the walkway, so people had to move out of the way. He kept his music blasting as people tried cursing him out. I was laughing so hard, until we eventually made it out and ended up on the highway, cruising 285, heading north.

"So, why you want me to spend the night all of a sudden?" I asked, seeing him smile as he leaned back in his seat to the side, one hand on the steering wheel as he glanced at me. I smirked. "Nah, nigga, don't get cute with me. Why you want me to spend the night?"

"I mean, you possibly the mother of my child," he said, shrugging innocently. "I don't want you to see me as this bad nigga that tricked you into sleeping with me."

I stayed quiet, just looking at him. He was so . . . damn. Why did he have to cut his dreads off?

"It is what it is, Jahiem," was all I said, looking out the window, watching the cars flow by on the highway.

When he got off the highway, we were entering the city of Dunwoody. I didn't even think someone like him would live here, but damn. We pulled up to these high-rise-like buildings, each unit having a metal balcony. He had to type in a code to get into the gated community, then pull into the parking garage just below the lofts.

"This is where you stay, Mr. I'm-a-thug-nigga, fuck-everybody, I'll-put-a-hole-in-your-chest-nigga? What are you doing in Dunwoody?" I asked with a laugh.

"I mean, I'm going to stay true to myself regardless, but when you make money to get out of a fuck situation, you place yourself in a better one. Not trying to stay in the hood forever.

Eventually want to move into a house, but I was waiting on a girl to come into my life for all that shit," he said, getting out.

I followed him up the steps and down the open hallways until we stopped at a door. "My shit is a little messy, so give me a minute to clean everything up," he said, opening the door. I rolled my eyes as I pushed past him to walk inside. "I'm serious—"

Cutting the light on, I looked around, seeing it was fucking spotless in here. Maybe a shirt was hanging on the back arm of a couch, but that was it. It was so nice in here I almost didn't want to touch anything. Three large windows with no blinds overlooked the city. There were black couches, black carpet, gray walls with a sound system and a flat-screen TV. His dining room was decorated nicely by the side of the door, and the kitchen was huge, with everything in its place.

"Jahiem, this is really nice," I told him, taking in the smell. It smelled like a man lived here. It was a clean, masculine-like smell that I was loving.

"Take yo' shoes off for me," he said, kicking his off.

I did as told while placing my stuff on the table. I walked down the hallway into his huge bedroom. He had a king-size bed with black sheets, covers, and pillows. A bookshelf was up against the wall with baby pictures. A flat-screen TV was hooked up, black rug on the floor, and the bathroom . . . Don't even get me started on the bathroom. Everything was neat and in order.

"This is really nice," I told him with a smile as I looked back at him.

"Yeah," he said, looking around, trying to be humble about it. "You the first girl to come in here, so be grateful."

"Nigga, how many girls you told that to?" I asked, and he laughed, rubbing his head.

"Nah, for real. I don't bring girls here. I got another spot for all of that."

"Mm-hmm, I bet," I mumbled. "Can I take a shower?"

"Yeah, go 'head. All the shit you need is in here," he said, pointing at the closet. "I'm out here about to put in some work real quick. Let me know if you want to eat something."

"Okay."

I took a shower, loving the shower head. I thought about what I knew was going to happen tonight between Jahiem and me. We were going to have sex. He didn't invite me to spend the night just to sleep, and I didn't come over here just to talk. I just didn't know what the fuck was going to happen after that. What did that do for us and this child?

When I was done, I slipped on a red basic shirt of his, barely covering my thighs, as I re-braided my hair with Porscha on speakerphone. The door to the room was closed, so hopefully he couldn't hear me.

"So, I mean, y'all fucking?" Porscha asked, and I laughed, looking at myself in the mirror, makeup free, clean face, body smelling good. I had no bra or panties on since I didn't have a spare. I slick checked this nigga's shit to look for any feminine products.

"I guess we are, girl. I don't know," I admitted. "If we do, it doesn't change nothing."

"Bitch, that changes everything! Girl, if you have sex with yo' baby daddy and he start giving it to you good, you are not going to want to share that nigga. He probably think because you pregnant you not going to fuck nobody else. Niggas nowadays search for pregnant pussy since it's supposed to be the best."

"Porscha, you need to stop." I laughed at her silly ass. "If we do sleep with each other again, I'm going to put the moves on him once again. He's not going to know what hit him. Him fucking other girls won't even compare to my ass."

"You better let it be known," she chimed in just as the door opened. He walked in, shirtless, texting on his phone as Porscha continued. "You better suck that nigga's dick like it's no tomorrow—"

"Porscha stop—"

"No, if you like him, which I think you do, because you wouldn't be over there if you didn't. I know you like I know myself, trick. You need to learn how to keep him. Suck that nigga's dick. Ride him like—"

"Oh my God," I groaned, seeing Jahiem smirking in the mirror. "Porscha, stop talking, like right now." I laughed. "This nigga is hearing everything you're saying."

"Nah, keep telling her what she gotta do," Jahiem said as I quickly turned around, throwing a washcloth at him.

"Oh, my bad, girl." She laughed. "Let me let y'all two kids go. I got a date with my boo anyway." She hung up just like that.

I looked at Jahiem, blushing bright red. I was so embarrassed, but I tried to play it off like it was nothing.

"Who told you to put my shirt on?" he asked, eyes roaming as I walked past him. I knew he saw a peek of the ass every time I moved.

"Nigga, I wasn't going to be walking around naked in your place, Jahiem." I sat back on the comfortable bed. Damn, this shit was plush. I made sure my weave was braided down tight as I put my scarf back on my head. Pulling the covers over my body, I felt the warmth of the sheets hit my ass and inner thighs. I didn't care if my legs were spread since I was covered. I was definitely in for the night. Grabbing the remote, I popped the TV on, and just like that, I was flipping through channels like it was my place. He continued to just stare at me, jeans hanging low, showing off that V cut and red boxer briefs.

"What, Jahiem?" I asked with a small laugh.

"You laying all up in my shit like this is yo' place."

I just stared at him, licking my lips before focusing back on the screen. I hadn't had a chance to see this episode of *Bad Girls Club*.

"And you ignoring me," he mumbled as he stepped into the bathroom, closing the door. I heard the shower going, and I just quietly listened. When he stepped back out, I nearly came on myself as he rubbed a small towel on his head, stepping in front of the counter that held the huge mirror. Nigga was butt-ass naked. He was a light-bright nigga with that strong, muscular back, ripped thighs, and white-ass feet. All he needed to do was to turn . . . He walked over to his closet, and that dick—Lord Jesus, shit was hanging low on soft.

"You need to put some clothes on, Jahiem," I mumbled as he walked back out, rubbing his body with lotion. I quickly looked away, seeing him smirk.

"You in my place. I sleep naked, and I walk around like this all the time." He laughed, cutting the lights off.

The TV was the only source of light as he walked to the edge of the bed, looking down at me. My heart was beating so fast I could barely breathe. It was happening. I knew we were going to have sex the moment I had agreed to come over here. I just didn't understand why I was so nervous all of a sudden. Body was on point. I look good naked, and I fucked like a champion, so why was I nervous to even be close to him like that?

"Jahiem, what are you doing?" I asked quickly, seeing him lift the covers up as he slipped underneath. I didn't have time to react when I felt that mouth on my thigh. He dragged that tongue up my thigh, sliding the shirt up as he let it travel to my stomach, hitting my breast as he popped his head up from the covers, body in between mine. We were face to face, eye to eye, as we stared at each other. My body was throbbing, already craving him.

"You know my name?" he asked softly. I nodded, eyes never leaving his. "What is it?"

"Jahiem," I barely whispered as he leaned in and kissed my neck softly.

"Say my whole name," he said, kissing my collarbone.

"Jahiem Carter," I let out.

He looked at my face again before leaning down and kissing me on the lips, just a light peck as he looked at me again.

"I'm so nervous," I admitted softly, and he smiled, kissing me again.

He relaxed his body against mine as my hands gripped his strong, thick back.

"Why you nervous?" he asked, looking me in the eyes.

I swallowed a huge gulp of nerves as I matched his stare. "'Cause," I started in a low voice, "you might end up hurting me." That was the truth. I hoped he knew I wasn't talking physically, either. My emotions could easily fall into his grip. We were having a baby together. Despite how we started, I already shared a connection with this man.

He just kissed me on my lips again. "I won't ever hurt you, Tiana," he said, using my full name. "Mother of my unborn child. I will never hurt you emotionally, nor physically. You are a part of me now. Anybody fuck with you, they fucking with me. Anybody step to you, they stepping to me. That's my word," he stated. "You understand?" I nodded. "Say my name one more time," he commanded, kissing my chest.

"Why?" I asked.

"Because I want you to know who you fucking this time," he said before taking a nipple in his mouth. My head went back as I moaned. "What's my name?"

"Jahiem Carter," I breathed, feeling his mouth travel down to my belly button. I remember that being his spot, but I just discovered that it was mine as well. I gripped his body with my thighs as his tongue dipped in and out, circled, and glided across my button before going lower.

"Better not be fucking nobody else but me from now on," he let out, and I nodded, feeling his legs spread my thighs wider. I was already wet. I was already throbbing and swelling up by the second, but that tongue, nigga . . . Took me over the edge. Sexually, I'd never been attracted to another man like Jahiem before in my life. I started begging for that pipe, pleading for that shit, and when he finally decided to give it to me, I was done.

Sliding in slow as he looked down at himself, he grunted slowly in response, closing his eyes. "Shit, you . . . feel like . . . " he started, words drifting off as he started to stroke with a steady force.

I knew I was loud as fuck, because he had to kiss me, keeping my mouth covered to shut me up. I told him deeper, nigga pushed further in; I said faster, he hit me at an angle on a faster stroke speed. Whatever spot he was hitting, I told him "Right there. Keep going." My body was trembling, muscles were clenching his dick harder before letting everything out on him just as he came in me, pushing as far as he could go and holding it.

"Jahiem," I breathed, wiping his forehead as he kissed me. I knew this was going to change everything about our relationship from two people having a baby to something more. I couldn't let no other bitch have his dick after me, though. Damn sure couldn't. So, I gently pushed him on his back as I straddled him. He was tired but already hard again, waiting for round two.

"You gonna do me how you did it last time, baby?" he asked, tongue hanging out in a teasing grin. "Do what yo' homegirl said—"

"Nigga, hush," I pressed, gripping his jaw, forcing him to look at me. "You better not let no other bitch get this dick after me."

"I won't as long as you take care of it," he said in a low voice.

We stared at each other as I gripped that chin tighter before kissing him on the lips, sealing the agreement we'd just created.

Realization

Jordyn

"So, he said what?" Rita asked, mouth dropped as she helped me move my things into my new place. I had grabbed a small two-bedroom house with Rita, just behind the schoolyard with the help of my parents, the university, and the money I made from playing my violin. I definitely didn't plan on staying on campus anymore. I had gone from becoming an instant celebrity for dating a Carter boy to getting my ass beat. Everyone had something to say about Jordyn. I hadn't seen Tia or Jade since, and now that it was homecoming weekend, with today being the football game, everyone was busy trying to get hype. Like I said in the beginning of the story, I rarely partook in school activities. They were pointless and a waste of time if you ask me. Same thing every year: marching band cuts up on the yard, Greeks walk around like colorful royalty, and the average students like us watch in awe. Not me, not ever.

So, now it was a Saturday afternoon, and after coming back from L.A. with Elijah a day ago, I was completely exhausted, but I felt like I was getting back to my old self once again.

"Jordyn, are you listening?" Rita asked as I turned to look at her, pushing my glasses up. We stood in our living room, boxes everywhere, trying to unpack in our new place.

"I am listening," I told her, looking at my best friend as she tied her long braids up.

"That nigga isn't no good for you anyway. I told you he be hitting me up on the low all the time, trying to fuck," she said as my eyes grew wide. She nodded slowly. "Girl, Elijah is a ho, and he will always be a ho. Not saying that he didn't like you, but he's one of those niggas that won't know what he had until it's gone, so you need to put distance between the two of you. Y'all being so close isn't healthy anyway if you're not in a serious relationship," she stated, and I nodded in agreement.

"I know," I told her, feeling my phone vibrate in my back pocket. Speak of the devil and he calls. Looking at the screen, I decided to answer. I didn't want things to be awkward between Elijah and me. I still very much enjoyed his company, but it was time that I did me.

"Hello?" I smiled, hearing the loud music being turned down.

"What's good with ya, baby? You like yo' new place? I told you to send me pictures of that shit and the address so I can stop by and give you a housewarming gift."

"It's so junky in here though, Elijah," I complained as Rita signaled for me to hang up the phone, looking pissed. I just waved her off as I stepped over the boxes, heading to my room on the right side. All that lay in there were two mattresses stacked on top of each other, my violin case sitting in the corner, and a huge oval-shaped mirror in another corner. This would have to do for now.

"You at the house now? Why you not at the game? I keep seeing niggas tweet about this shit. Supposed to be one big-ass party at the stadium right now."

"You know I'm not into that stuff." I sighed, sitting on my mattress, looking at my dingy nails. "You're not on your way over here, are you?"

"I am." Elijah laughed, honking the horn at someone. "Aye, move the fuck out the way! Shit! Niggas can't drive worth a fucking damn, bruh!" he snapped suddenly. "Yo, I'm by the school now. Where do I turn at?"

As soon as I told him the directions to my place, I hung up feeling like I'd just failed myself. What was all that shit I spewed out earlier about distancing myself and doing me? Now the man was on his way over here? I quickly looked at myself. My face was still bruised, but it was getting better with time. My curly black hair was pulled back in a simple ponytail, and I wore slacks with an oversized T-shirt.

Stepping back into the living room, I saw Rita sitting on a box. She gave me that knowing look.

"He's coming over here, isn't he?" she asked, and I nodded with a smile, shrugging. "Okay, bitch, you'll learn when I tell you he's no good for you."

"I'll be okay. He said what he had to say, and so did I."

She rolled her eyes just as his infamous black truck pulled up, music blasting. I looked through the screen door, seeing him step out, pulling up his straight-leg jeans, locs moving about as he walked with his typical strut up to the steps. He was wearing an over-the-top dramatic colorful sweater that looked like it should be worn only in the '80s, black jeans, with matching high yellow, pink, and blue Jordans to go with the sweater. I couldn't describe his fashion sense.

It was usually whatever he felt like wearing. His chains were swinging, with his tongue sitting on top of his lower lip. He smiled as we stared at each other through the door before he opened it.

"Shawty, you got a spot smacked down in the middle of the fucking hood!" He laughed, walking over to me, completely ignoring Rita.

"Hello to you too, Elijah," I greeted softly, pushing my glasses up as he wrapped his arms around me, kissing my neck.

"Damn, I missed yo' nerdy ass," he said against my ear, hand gripping my booty, causing me to laugh.

"Mmmph," Rita let out with a smack of her teeth as she walked back to her room, slamming the door. We both watched the dramatic exit before he turned back to me, eyeing my hair.

"What's wrong with yo' homegirl?" he asked with a laugh, taking my hair down, combing through it with his hand. Elijah was definitely a hair man. You know some guys are into booty, legs, boobs, etc? Elijah Carter loved long hair. That was his fetish. We could be having sex, and if my hair didn't get pulled, I wasn't doing something right.

"You being here is her problem. She says you're no good for me," I told him, looking him in the eyes as he smirked at me.

"I'm not. I tell you that shit all the time, though." He laughed. "Shit, my brothers tell me that shit all the time when they ask about you."

"She also says you try to talk to her," I stated sternly, giving him a look. I knew he was going to do him regardless, but I felt like we were past the point of having sex with friends.

"Shit, I already hit it." He shrugged, walking to my room. "One time was enough for me. I wasn't feeling her like that."

I felt my heart drop at the thought of them having sex behind my back. He just so freely admitted it, while she flat-out lied. Taking a deep breath, I felt myself putting my emotions in check before closing the door behind me as I walked in the room.

When he turned to look at me, his smile dropped and his face got serious. "She didn't tell you?"

"No, but it's cool. You are free to do whoever you want." I smiled sweetly.

"I know." He smirked, backing me up against the wall, hands coming to my waist to pull me closer to him. "You still my main, Jordyn. Nobody can replace you, especially not in sex. Shit, I have a hard time fucking bitches now without thinking about what the fuck you doing." He laughed.

"Where's my gift?" I asked, wanting to change the subject before I got sick. He just looked down at me and smiled before bending down to pick me up from the waist, causing me to shriek in surprise. "What are you doing, Elijah?" I laughed, wrapping my legs around him.

"Giving you yo' gift," he stated, taking me to the bed.

Of course, my scary behind didn't even confront Rita about having sex with Elijah. At this point, I didn't care. I was over this emotional bullshit that I'd allowed myself to succumb to.

Later on that night, after unpacking, I just decided last minute to attend a party that Rita was invited to. I never questioned the people that she knew, but somehow she seemed to be hip to all the cool things happening in the city. So, Rita and I got dressed and stepped out for the night. A girl's night out, if you will. My hair was straightened, hitting my waist. I wore an all-black dress with heels, gold jewelry, and light makeup. I could still feel the bruises from the beat down I'd received, but what was the point in dwelling on it and hiding from society after a setback, you know? Fuck it. I was young; I could be hot when I wanted to, was passing all my classes with As, and I had the best sex game in this world—definitely in this book, for sure.

So, the party we pulled up at was somebody's huge house. Someone in the music industry, I'm not sure who, was having a music release party. A lot of rappers, singers, models, and people wanting to come up in the industry were there. I just wanted to have a good time, get a drink in my hand, and find someone for the night. The freak side of me was out and ready to stay.

Walking with Rita, following her down to the basement with my cup in hand, I knew I caught the eyes of the guys in there. Even if they were with a girl, their eyes were on me, wondering who I was. Some were wondering if I was with Elijah, and a few were not caring either way. The music was pumping throughout the house as we stepped down into the huge, smoke-filled basement.

"She's cute!" Rita yelled over the music as she pointed at a stud who was leaned up against the corner, eyeing me hard. I'd never been into studs. If I wanted to have sex with a man, I would have sex with a man, not a woman trying to be a man. It was pointless. Sadly, I usually attracted studs. Rarely did I get a girl who was comfortable being a woman and nothing more.

"You can have her," I told Rita, whose eyes lit up at that statement.

I let my eyes scan the room before feeling a hand touch my lower back. I turned around to see this tall, light-skin guy standing there, taking a pull on his blunt as he smiled at me. He had low-cut dark brown hair, slanted dark brown eyes, plump lips made for kissing, and a body that could rival Elijah's any day. There was not a tattoo in sight. I licked my lips slowly as I smiled. *Let's see if we have a winner for the night.*

"What's good, ma?" he asked, Northern accent heavy. "You look like you don't belong with these ratchet broads at this party."

"How can you tell?" I smirked, and he smiled.

He kicked himself off the wall as he stood directly in front of me, leaning in close to my ear as he licked his lips. "They call me JB," he stated against my ear, and I felt my body send off chills as I smiled to myself. *Body knows what the mind wants; no room for a heart to fuck it up with emotions.*

"I'm Jordyn," I told him as he looked me over slowly. We just stared at each other, taking in what was in front of us before I gripped the front part of his jeans to pull him closer, licking my lips again. "Can we get out of here?" I asked, and his eyes lit up.

"Where you tryna go?" he asked with a smile. I shrugged. He understood. No words were needed.

Next thing I knew, we were in his car, back seats down, with me riding him like my own personal horse. My dress was hiked up, booty bouncing, hair whipping, as he held on, matching me thrust for thrust. My phone lay beside him as it lit up with Elijah's picture flashing on the screen. I smiled before turning the phone over, continuing to enjoy my ride. *Fuck him. He's been doing him, it's been time to do me.*

When I finally did make it home, Elijah had texted me several times and called me back to back. It had to be at least three in the morning, with everyone still out partying and enjoying the nightlife of Atlanta, when I decided to call him back. I was already laying in the bed, freshly showered, with a notebook in my hand, writing music for the violin.

"Hello?" he answered, sounding irritated.

"I'm sorry I missed your calls," I told him, pushing my glasses up. I didn't bother to read his text messages because half the time, I couldn't understand what he was saying anyway. I was still trying to get the hang of texting, let alone learn all this slang and acronyms.

"You was at the mixtape release party for one of my homeboys," he said, no smile in his voice whatsoever.

"I'm not really sure, Rita was invited, so I just tagged along with her." I yawned, putting my books aside as I got up to cut off the light. "You have people spying on me now, Elijah?"

"Nah, fuck nah. You know I don't, Jordyn," he snapped, and I cocked my head back, wondering where this attitude was coming from. "Look, do what you wanna do. I know we not together, but be careful about that shit. If you fucking niggas the first time you meet them, make sure they wrap that shit up."

"Oh my God!" I shrieked. "You have people spying on me, Elijah? People running back to tell you—"

"You fucked a nigga on the first sight?" he screamed, setting off the very first argument we'd ever had. "Who do that shit? You don't know what the fuck these niggas got going on, and who—"

"Elijah! You do the same thing!" I retorted, sitting up in the bed. "You have sex with all these girls! You had sex with my best friend!"

"Nigga, she fucked me. That's different. I didn't come after her. She sent me naked pictures of her, shawty! Check yo' bitch; don't check me!"

"Get the fuck off my phone with this nonsense, Elijah. I'm tired, and—"

"So, when I called you, you was fucking who-ever?" he asked, voice chilled. I could hear the storm brewing in the calmness of his voice. Elijah can go from zero to one hundred to neg-ative twenty-three and back to five hundred in a matter of seconds.

"I was with someone, yes," I answered, push-ing my glasses up. "You—"

He hung up. I looked at my phone in utter shock. If he thought I was going to play into this childish game, trying to call him back or send him a text message, he was sadly mistaken. Right when I was about to cut the phone off, I saw an incoming text message from him.

SO U REALLY JUST ANOTHER HOE
AFTER ALL SHAWTY. U THE SAME LIKE
EVERY OTHER BITCH IN THE A.

I decided to call him back, taking the bait. I was about to let him have it as soon as he picked up the phone.

"Why you calling me, man?" Elijah groaned. "I'm not—"

"No! You said what the fuck you had to say, so now it's my turn. How dare you bitch to me about having sex with someone else—"

"I'm saying, though, you just fucked me earlier today! I don't know no bitch that do shit like that unless she's a fucking ho!"

"Elijah, you slept with my best friend. Whether or not she came at you, you slept with the only other person that is closest to me. She has a piece of you that you and I share!" I cried, letting my emotions finally take over. "You didn't see me go off on you. I didn't call you a ho or tell you off. You don't think that shit hurts? No telling how many other girls you have sex with before or after me!"

He stayed quiet as I wiped my face, hating that he brought me to fucking tears. Fuck it. I just hung the phone up and turned it off altogether.

I couldn't even lay the fuck down when my door opened and the lights popped on. Rita stood there looking like she was woken out of sleep, eyes squinting bad.

"Girl, what are you yelling about in here? Who are you on the phone with? It better not be Elijah," she snorted before actually looking at my face. Her smile disappeared as I just stared at her, hoping to make her ass uncomfortable.

"So, you slept with him?" I asked, and her eyes grew wide before shifting to the floor, and her hands were nervously moving about.

"You said I could," was all she said.

Looking at my only friend that I ever had in this city, I just lay down on the mattress, turning over as I pulled the covers over me.

"Close my door and turn the lights off on your way out," was all I could manage to say.

Sunday morning was supposed to be a relaxing day. I had rehearsal with my orchestra on the yard later in the afternoon, I planned on keeping to myself. Unfortunately, I woke up irritated and had a serious headache from last night's argument with Elijah. Laying down on the mattress, I grabbed my phone off the floor to cut it on. The guy from last night apparently wanted to hang out, take me out to eat, and, I guess, see me again. I wasn't interested, though. I had just wanted sex, that was it. Sure enough, Elijah's text messages filled my inbox shortly after, with apology after apology. I dialed my voicemail to see what he had left me since he was now in his right mind.

"Aye, Jordyn, turn yo' fucking phone on, man." He sighed into the phone. "I'm sorry about how I acted and for what I said. You know I didn't mean that shit about you being a ho, and fucking yo' friend was a mistake I will never make again, baby. Just . . . answer this damn phone. I fucked up, I know, but I'm not used to you dealing with other people besides me. So, my bad if I got upset, but I don't . . . I hate to even think about you with another nigga. I don't know how to take that." He sighed before the recording went off.

Looking at my phone, I just texted him a simple, I ACCEPT YOUR APOLOGY, and left it at that. I didn't want to speak on it again.

Flashback

Trent

I used to be bad as shit in high school. Every girl wanted to fuck with me, and every nigga tried to get like me. My sister Olivia and I were the most wanted people there. If Elijah showed up, then it was just the same. I remember one day, it was the last class before school let out in tenth grade, spring semester. I mean, we're talking back in the day when sagging your jeans was cool, and wearing long-ass T-shirts with the hats tipped up was considered thug as hell. Nah, not me. I was always on that pretty-boy style, ever since I could remember. I left all that hood shit to Elijah. I was in an English class, flirting with this pretty chick I'd been trying to get at for weeks. She was playing games, but her homegirls already told me she was feeling me. So, we were sitting in the back of the class, me wearing a fitted blue American Eagle shirt with some jeans and fresh white Vans. Yeah, I was on my white-boy shit. Told y'all, I been doing this. Hair was clean cut, hazel eyes were making the girls fall in love. I was that lover boy, fucking girl after girl since I lost my virginity in the seventh grade—Elijah and I both at the same time, same place.

"Any questions?" the teacher asked as I reached over to the side, tapping Nadine's caramel thigh. She smacked her teeth, rolling her eyes as she shifted in her seat. I couldn't take my eyes off those legs in that jean mini skirt, and she knew it, too. I bet she was slick trying to make that shit higher by spreading her legs in the seat. Girls do shit like that.

"Nadine," I whispered as she faced front. "Nadine," I whispered loudly, catching a few people turn around. "Aye, turn the fuck around. Nobody was talking to y'all."

"Trent, you have something to say?" the teacher asked just as the bell rang.

I smirked, hopping out of my desk with my books in hand. "Fuck nah," I let out, and the class laughed. Before the teacher could even call me out on it, I rushed out the classroom and down the hall, weaving in and out of the growing crowd of students.

"Trent!" a girl called out.

"Aye, bruh! We still playing basketball at the house?" Camp asked as I stopped to slap hands with him and a few of my homeboys.

"Hell yeah. I'm on the way there now. Shiloh is supposed to come get me," I said, watching the girls walk. I was always scanning the crowd for my next target. I was strong on not fucking with ugly, fat, and dark-skin bitches. I'd never been into them; didn't even like being around them. I was too good for that shit.

I spotted my sister, Olivia, with her clique, her followers, walking down the hall as people made room for them. Every nigga was trying to get in her pants, but her brothers had a tight lock on that. Nobody could get to her without going through us.

"Man, I swear yo' sister be looking on point more and more every day," Dion said, and the boys agreed.

"Don't tell her that shit," I cracked, eyeing her friends around her. Most of them I'd known since we were kids, but there was one she kept around that we all made fun of. She was the security bitch out of the group. Big Tay.

"Yo, look at what the fuck Big Tay got on," I pointed out as we all looked, seeing she had on a shirt, two sizes too small, with her jeans barely taking in her stomach. Bitch was big and wide and tall. A giant.

"Attention, students: buses 309 and 315 will be doing second load today and tomorrow. Buses 309 and 315," the announcement said before cutting off.

"She look like a fucking potato, walking potato," Dion joked, and we laughed, watching them walk closer to us.

Olivia stood there in her matching Baby Phat dress, purse, and shoes. She had dark skin with hazel eyes and long, pretty hair. She and I were more alike than her and Elijah. He was too busy trying to be like our older brother Shiloh.

"What y'all doing after school? We trying to go to the movies tonight," Olivia said, moving her hair off her shoulders as she popped on her gum, books sitting on her hips as she eyed my friends. All her homegirls looked on point but Big Tay. You know I had to say something.

"Tay, why the fuck every time I see you with my sister and her friends you gotta be the one that always stands out?" I started, and she rolled her eyes. I'd known Big Tay since we were kids. She and Olivia had been best friends for years, and we never got along.

"Nigga, do not start with me with yo' tight-ass shirt on," she snapped with a roll of her eyes, *trying to pop on her gum as cute as my sister did it.*

"Y'all two might as well go ahead and get married," Olivia joked, and we both gasped in disgust.

"I can't fuck with pretty niggas," she let out, looking me up and down with a smirk.

"Nah-uh. What did you say last night on the phone, ho?" Candice called out as the girls started talking and yelling at once. My eyes instantly grew at the thought of Tay even mentioning me on the phone with her friends. I never would have thought that.

"Y'all be talking about a nigga on the phone?" I laughed. "What she say?"

"Don't y'all dare say a word."

"She said she had a crush on you since y'all were in the first grade!" Alexis let out, and my mouth dropped. I could hear my homeboys laughing behind me, lockers closing as they started making their comments and jokes.

"I can't believe you told him!" Olivia let out.

I just stared at Tay, who couldn't even look at me, too busy going off on the girls. This chick, this big chick I'd known for years, many sleepovers, play fights, and arguments, had a crush on me? Why would she even think I would return that feeling? She was light-skin, but probably weighed more than all of us combined, with multiple chins, and probably always had food in her mouth or around it. She didn't know how to dress, and her hair was always in a messy-ass afro. Matter of fact, since I'd known her, she always dressed like a tomboy. If there was one thing that was a turn-off for me besides weight and complexion, it was dressing like a boy. Yet, when she did dress like a girl, it never worked out—like now, wearing a shirt that showed that light lump of meat hanging out the waist of her small-ass jeans. Shit was just disgusting. She had small, chinky-like eyes you could barely see because of her big-ass cheeks, and just overall she had no business liking a nigga like me. You feel me?

"You got a crush on me?" I repeated as she turned to look at me, eyes rolling, neck moving, full of attitude.

"I mean, you cute. That's all it was. They asked who did I think was cute at the school, and who I would fuck if I had the chance. I said you. Not yo' li'l punk-ass friends behind you cracking potato jokes like I can't hear them!" she snapped, and my boys fell silent.

I felt my cell phone ring in my pocket, and I saw it was Elijah calling me, probably to let me know he was outside.

"*Do you like her, Trent?*" Candice pressed, and Tay hit her in the arm to silence her.

"*Do not answer that,*" Olivia warned, cutting her hazel eyes at me.

"*Nah, I look at you like the sister I never wanted,*" I told Tay, and the girls tried to keep themselves from laughing. "*But you ain't got no business liking a nigga like me with the way you look, shawty. Facts!*"

"*Ohhhh!*" the boys yelled as I turned around, slapping hands with each of them.

"*Whale-looking-ass shawty, you might kill me in my sleep by rolling over on me. I can't fuck with you like that!*"

"*Daaayummm!*"

I felt like I was on a roll, not really caring if I was hurting her feelings. It was the attention and praise I was going for. When people stopped walking in the hallways to see what the commotion was about, I kept going, thinking this shit was cool. Tay was a big girl; she knew how to take it and brush it off. At least, I thought she did.

"*Nigga said she was a fucking whale!*" Camp repeated out loud.

"*You need to stop talking about my friend like that, Trent. I'm serious,*" Olivia warned, but I wasn't hearing it. A young nigga in high school looking for laughs, I thought I was the shit.

"Nah, big ol' two-size-too-small-clothes-wearing ass! Fuck you got on yo' little sister T-shirt for with yo' meat hanging out?" I let out as the crowd laughed, playfully tapping her stomach to make it jiggle.

Tay stayed silent, just watching me, looking me directly in my eyes as I kept going.

"Only way I could ever like you is if you looked like the rest of yo' friends in this group, shawty. Aye, bruh, what we say about Big Tay?" I asked, tapping my homeboy's arm.

"Big Tay is big security nigga," Chris stated, and we all laughed. "Shit, I might hire y'o ass."

"Stop it! I'm serious!" Olivia screamed, but the damage was done.

Tay just turned and walked away. It didn't matter to me, seeing them go after her. I didn't give a fuck at that moment. I was soaking up the attention.

When I went outside to meet up with my brother, I could see a crowd of girls all surrounding Shiloh's brand new 2007 Chevy Impala. The music was bumping, with Elijah in the passenger seat. I hopped in the back, already telling Elijah what had happened as he turned around to face me, short locs trying to grow, My big brother Shiloh was sitting in the driver seat, trying to talk to some senior high school girls who knew he was already in his early twenties. Both brothers were wearing long white tees, big-ass jeans with the Air Forces and gold chains. A wad of cash was sitting in Elijah's lap.

"You went in on Big Tay, nigga?" Elijah laughed as we slapped hands. "Where Livie at? She must got a ride?"

"Shit, I don't know," I said, shrugging as I pulled out my phone.

"Ah, I can't believe you went in on Big Tay. I wish I was there to see that shit."

"You should be in fucking school," I mumbled, knowing our grandmother wouldn't approve of him missing days in school to be on some thug shit.

"What I need school for when I can make money off the top?" E pressed, waving the wad of cash in my face. I immediately smacked his hand away. "Nigga, what?" he flipped jokingly as he punched me in my shoulder, causing a quick session of us trying to hit each other, getting a lick without getting hit back.

"Aye! Aye!" Shiloh snapped, looking back at us. "Y'all moving the fuck out of my car. Stop with that childish shit!"

We sat still, with him looking back at me, trying not to laugh.

"Bitch," he mumbled as I faked like I was going to hit him.

We assumed Olivia was going to stay over at her friend's house because she never answered the phone, so we kept on moving. It wasn't until later on that night that I popped into her room, trying to see if she could do my homework for me. Elijah was out with Shiloh once again, so it was always just her and me at the house. Grandma was asleep and Mama was at work. So, when I walked into her room, shirtless and wearing basketball shorts. I collapsed on her bed, and she flipped.

"Nigga, get off! You sitting on my books!" she snapped, trying to push me.

"Can you do my homework for me, twin?"

"No! The way you did Big Tay was wrong. You know she was crying, right?"

I sat up in the bed with all the seriousness, looking at my sister, hazel eyes matching mine.

"Yeah, you made her cry. She actually has been liking you for years. I always knew and never said anything about it. You just took it too far, though."

"Why would she like me?" I just didn't get that shit. Like, why do you like me? I gave you no reason, didn't flirt with you, and didn't even look at you like that.

"She just does," she said, shrugging, trying to push me off her bed. "Now she probably won't ever speak to you again."

"Yeah, right." I laughed. "If she took me serious today, then she didn't deserve to even like me in the first place, shawty."

Sure enough, that next day, Big Tay didn't speak a word to me, nor look in my direction. Even after I apologized, she never spoke another word to me since. I was cool with that, though. She was Olivia's friend. She was a friend of the family, but not a friend of mine, so it didn't hurt my feelings at the end of the day.

Only reason why I went through this long-ass flashback is because now my sister was moving out of Grandma's house. It was a Sunday afternoon, warm as fuck outside, too. Homecoming was officially over, so I was dealing with the aftermath of partying nonstop. Today was the day all of the brothers had to help Livie move into her new house in west Atlanta with her roommate. Who the fuck was her roommate? None other than Big Tay. I hadn't seen her since high school graduation. Even then, I barely noticed her anymore since she'd stopped talking to me. Olivia still kept in contact with her, and I guess she moved out of state for school and was now moving back after getting hired somewhere here in Atlanta. I wondered if she was still on the same no-speaking bullshit even now that we were grown.

Shit. I glanced at the time, seeing it was going on one o'clock in the afternoon as I drove through the west side of Atlanta, smell of Jade throughout my car like a mixture of weed and flowers. It was a big turn-off when a female, especially a girl I was claiming as my own, smelled like weed, but she got me back into smoking it more and more, so I couldn't blame her completely.

I felt my phone vibrate in my lap, and I glanced to see who was calling, eyes shifting from road to screen and back again.

"Yo?" I answered, already hearing the loud music being turned down.

"Aye, where the fuck is this shit at again? She said it's in Marietta?" Elijah asked into the phone, loud as always. Even though he was still mad at me about his girl getting dropped by mine, we decided to let the females handle that. Only thing we could do was keep them apart.

"I don't know. I'm just following my GPS," I told him, making a turn down a wooded street. Small brick houses decorated each side as I saw myself getting closer and closer to her address.

It wasn't the hood where she stayed, but it definitely wasn't the best of the best. Yet, for her first time moving out, Olivia did good. "Where you at, E?"

"Shit, I don't know, bruh. I'm just going to say fuck it, turn back around, and go back to bed," he complained with a sigh. "Don't feel like lifting boxes and shit no way."

"Aye, she told you who her roommate was?" I asked with a small laugh as I pulled up to the side of the house, already seeing Jahiem and Talin standing outside with Olivia, talking. Her house was a small, two-bedroom brick house with a fenced-in backyard and a basement. Shit looked beat down, with bars on the windows, but overall, she had her own place. A lot of people couldn't say the same thing.

I spotted a black Toyota parked in the dirt driveway that I didn't recognize and immediately thought about Big Tay.

"Aye, you hear me?" E snapped into the phone as I turned the car off. I almost forgot I was on the phone.

"Nah, what you say?"

"Nigga, fuck it. Who is her roommate?"

"Big Tay," I stated, and he laughed outright, causing me to laugh. "Bruh, I don't even think she would want us to call her Big Tay."

"Ahhh, shit! Now I gotta come so I can see her ass! I didn't even know her and Olivia were still friends." E laughed harder. "Damn, text me the address. I'm stopping to get me something eat. Whatever address Jahiem gave me is wrong."

"A'ight," I said before hanging up. So, you know yo' boy had to show out a little bit. I knew I was going to see her today, so I'd dressed for the occasion. Not that it mattered, but when you see someone from your past, you want to make sure they see you as a grown-ass man. She had a crush on me back then? Wait until she saw me now.

I looked in the mirror, licking my lips before stepping out of the car wearing my Ray Bans, fresh cut from yesterday morning, and diamond stud earrings in each ear. I had on a basic white V-neck Polo shirt with a vintage jean jacket, Diesel jeans, brown Polo boots, minimal accessories, and yo' boy smelled good. I kept it simple, but simple works best for me, because I know the face is where I get most of the girls at anyway. Like I said earlier in the book, I don't step out that bathroom without looking good. Call me a pretty boy all you want. I believe in being, looking, and feeling clean.

"Pretty-boy T!" Jahiem joked as I walked over, smiling hard while looking back at the black Toyota, pointing.

"Whose car is that?" I pressed as Olivia smirked, hazel eyes beaming.

"You know who," she let out, and I laughed. "She's inside putting her stuff in her room now. You should go speak."

"Oh, so she's speaking to me now?"

"Oh, yeah. I forgot about you and that girl falling out," Talin said before laughing. "What did y'all used to call her?"

"Big Tay," I stated and laughed while slapping hands with Jahiem. "AKA, Big Take-yo'-food-from-you-while-you-not-looking."

"You ain't right, Trent," Olivia concluded with a shake of her head.

Just as she said it, another truck pulled up, and out hopped Elijah's wild ass, talking about he was lost. The only people missing were Ontrell, Anthony, and Shiloh.

"Where Big Tay at?" Elijah asked, walking up toward us as we all greeted him. Dreads were wild in his face as he adjusted his jacket. He was my complete opposite in every aspect. He and Jahiem were more alike in personality, than he and I were. We all stood out there for a few minutes, remembering the past, before Olivia finally stepped in.

"Y'all don't need to continue to call her that. Tay or Taylor is fine," Olivia corrected as she turned to walk back to the house. "Come see my new place. Come on! I want to give you guys a tour. I have furniture that has to be moved, and Grandma said she's going to let me have her old china cabinet." We followed our sister into the house, some of us ducking as we entered the small but cozy two-bedroom shoebox.

As soon as we stepped in, the living room was immediately there, with a small hallway going straight back, dipping off into three rooms. The kitchen was on the left side, with a door leading to the basement. There was no dining room. Mattresses were laid up against the wall, tables and chairs were stacked and out of place, with the TV still in the box. The carpet was a dark green. I'd never seen no shit like that before.

I could hear music blasting from one of the back rooms, and I smirked. Big Tay. Taking my jacket and shades off, I set them down on the couch that was waiting to be moved.

"Y'all wanna see the basement?" Olivia asked excitedly, walking toward the door.

"Man, you gonna let us throw you a house party weekend after next for our birthday?" E asked, following our sister to the door.

I hung back a little as they walked down to the lower level, and instead walked toward the back rooms, curious. I could hear Tay singing along to Beyoncé. Hell if I knew what song. I just knew it was Beyoncé. So, walking closer to her room, I stopped just shy of the entrance and poked my head in. I nearly dropped to the floor when I got a glimpse of her. She stood there with her back facing me, looking at the wall in thought. She wore a T-shirt and shorts with the word Pink going across it, her hair was in a high, huge afro ball on top of her head. She placed her hand on her hip, moving to the song as I eyed her caramel-colored body. She'd lost weight. She was still thick, but it wasn't . . . damn.

Shit, I couldn't even think. My dick was trying to bust through my jeans the more I looked at her. Big Tay . . . I smiled to myself, looking her over once more. She had gold bangles lined up on each arm as she moved closer to the wall, barefooted, with pretty toes painted in red. She still had hips and an ass that could make a man go crazy. Bodywise, she was still bigger than what I liked, only because I liked slim girls, but she was definitely sexy with it. She would have no problem getting a nigga if she didn't already have one.

But what did her face look like? The moment I had that thought, she turned around and froze as her eyes locked with mine. I smiled slowly.

She didn't, for the first few seconds, and I didn't know I was holding in my own damn breath until she smiled back.

"Hi," she mouthed shyly over the music before grabbing her phone off the desk, cutting it off.

I couldn't respond. Just looked her over slow, like it was my last time I was going to ever see her. Still had those chinky-like eyes with a slant, and cute, puffy cheeks, but her face had matured into a sexy woman. Her pink lips naturally poked out like she was ready to be kissed, and she had no extra chin, none of that. She definitely didn't look like the same Big Tay from our childhood.

Before I could even say anything, I felt a hand clamp down on my shoulder as E walked around me to walk into the room like it was his.

"Daaaaayuummm! Big Tay!" Elijah screamed while rushing up to hug her. She laughed, arms around his neck. "Shawty, look at you! You sexy as fuck! What happened?"

"Shut up, Elijah." She laughed as the rest of the boys came in, showing the same excitement about her new look.

I looked down before glancing at Olivia, who watched me closely, eyes squinting.

"What, Livie?"

"Nothing." She smirked cutely with a shrug.

No one could get over how Taylor looked. Even when Ontrell showed up, he was floored, acting out just as bad as Elijah. I didn't have any words. I felt like I had to get to know her all over again, even though none of the older brothers were as close to her as E, Livie, and I were.

Walking back to the living room, texting Jade, I felt someone come up from behind me.

"So, you and her still not speaking?" Elijah asked, smirking hard at me as he flipped his locs back from his face.

"Nigga, get the fuck on, bruh. It's not even like that," I snapped quietly as he laughed.

"Aye, I know she not yo' type, but even you gotta admit she's fine as fuck. Body for days. You seen her ass, though?"

"Elijah," I started, stating his full name so he knew I wasn't trying to be fucked with.

"All I'm saying is she looks ten times better than the bitch you fucking with now," he said, hands up in the air. "All I'm saying. Better hit it before another nigga do."

I watched him walk out the door then I looked back, seeing Taylor talking with Ontrell, laughing it up. She glanced at me, and we locked eyes for a second before she turned her attention back to Trell.

That Old Thang

Taylor

The Pretty Girl

"Ooooh! I'm so excited!" I shrieked as we watched the movers bring the furniture into the new house. I had just moved back home to Atlanta from L.A. and couldn't contain my excitement at the thought of truly being on my own at twenty-four. It was the best feeling in the world.

So, my story is pretty interesting. I'm sure by now you know the history between the Carter boys and me. I pretty much grew up with them, especially Elijah, Olivia, and Trent. Their grandma was like a grandma to me, their mother was a second mom to me, and their dad? Well, that's a long story, but I remember the fallout between the boys and their dad. Not my story to tell. Anyway, back to me. So, yeah, my name is Taylor. Back then, I was that little chubby girl who always used to get into fights, stayed eating, stayed talking shit and trying to hang with the boys. Hold up. Don't get it fucked up. Just because I grew some doesn't mean I don't know how to fuck a bitch up. I just kept that side of myself on the low, unless I felt like I was being tried. Only then would Big Tay from back in the day come out of me.

My best friend, my ride or die, my sister for life, Olivia Carter was the only girl to have my back and to know everything there is to know about me. Us moving in together may have been a bad idea, but we knew each other so well that problems that other friends would have while living together wouldn't be an issue for us. She knew I liked space; I knew she liked privacy. Simple. We respected each other and knew when to back the fuck away when things got heated.

"So, are you ready to see my brother?" Olivia asked as the last mover walked out of our house. I looked at her with a smirk before rolling my eyes. "I'm serious! You haven't spoken to him since high school. Will you be okay if Trent comes?"

"Girl," I said, waving her off as I sat down on the red couch. Boxes were everywhere in the living room. Furniture and mattresses, bed frames, and artwork were lined up against the wall, ready to be placed. Today was going to be a long-ass day. "I am too old to be worried about some high school mess. It's petty," I told her, and she smiled.

"Well, good, because they're all supposed to be on their way soon to help us move these things," she said, looking around.

We locked eyes, slowly smiling before screaming in excitement at the thought of us living together.

"Okay," she started, putting her hair in a ponytail. "Let's do what we can so they can have space to move this stuff."

So, for the next hour, we pushed boxes into our rooms, Beyoncé blasting from my phone as we sang along to the songs. I attempted to set up my bed in my room but failed miserably. I wasn't good with all this fixing shit. Somehow, don't know when it happened, but I had become the biggest girly-girl—heels, dresses, skirts, makeup, and had to have my nails done. It was a must.

Walking into the bathroom to check my face, I smiled. Yeah, I was excited to see Trent for the simple fact that I hadn't seen him since school days. He was fine. Lord knows he was fine back then; I could only imagine what he looked like now. Elijah was cute in his own wild way, but Trent was . . . I closed my eyes slowly, letting a smile creep on my face. I just remembered that model-like, baby-boy face with those hazel eyes, always dressed preppy. In an all-black school, he stood out. I wondered what he was going to think when he saw me. I had lost weight; was still losing, actually. I worked out and ate healthy for the most part. I kept my stomach flat enough, just leaving the hips and booty that constantly got me attention. I'm not saying I had the best body in the world, but it was definitely shapely, and I was comfortable with it. Whatever. I was getting sidetracked again. I had come into the bathroom to change because it was getting hot—and to secretly show off my legs and booty. I knew a group of boys were coming to the house, so why not look cute? I slipped on a T-shirt and my Victoria's Secret Pink shorts and walked into my room, looking around.

My natural dark, curly hair was pushed up in a cute 'fro ball on my head as I jammed to "Grown Woman." Beyoncé was that bitch. For any occasion, she was that bitch that always put me in a good mood. I had pictures I wanted to put up, a closet I needed to organize, and so much I had to do.

"Hey, I think some of them are already here," Olivia said over the music as she popped in and out of my room. I started to follow her out but decided I was already warm inside the house. I didn't feel like putting on any pants. Walking back in, I started to fill my closet up with my boxes of shoes, sneakers, heels, and flats. I have a shoe fetish. Clearly.

I was eyeing the wall closest to the window as I thought about what I wanted to put on there. Smiling to myself as I crossed my arms over my chest, I thought about Trent again. I thought about how I used to have the biggest crush on my best friend's brother. I think it started when I was eleven years old. I mean, I always thought he was cute, but my attraction to boys didn't kick in until middle school.

It was a Friday night, and I was spending the night at Olivia's house for the weekend. I wasn't much to look at back then, but I had attitude, and I had heart. So, I was in Olivia's room, looking through magazines at outfits, talking about what boys we thought were cute at school. We had just finished up a session of trying to pop our asses in the mirror together—what the kids call twerking now.

We were sitting on her bed in long T-shirts with our hair wrapped up in scarves when Elijah's boney, dark-skin ass walked in. He was shirtless, wearing just his jeans and socks. His hair was low cut, with those low, droopy-looking eyes I used to make fun of, calling him a hound dog. The nigga was a li'l thug.

"Aye," he said, walking in as he pulled his jeans up. "Where Mama put that food at? I don't see it in the fridge, Livie."

"We already ate it, nigga," I retorted, and we both laughed.

He squinted his eyes at me just as Trent came walking in behind him, light skin with those hazel eyes bright, same low-cut hair, shirtless and showing off his bird chest. They didn't look alike, but their actions and mannerisms were the same. Olivia looked like Elijah in a prettier, girlier way, but she had Trent's hazel eyes.

"Man, why you always gotta fucking be here, Big Tay?" Elijah snapped, and I rolled my eyes, smacking my teeth.

"Because I can, nigga. You got a problem with it?" I let out as I stood up from the bed, large shirt hanging like a dress, stomach poking through.

"Mama said she can stay the weekend, so get out of my room! Boys ain't allowed to be in here

anyway," Olivia quipped as they walked right on in, Trent smirking hard at me.

"What you looking at with yo' ugly self?" I snapped as he glanced at Elijah, who smiled in response. Without warning, they came straight toward us, grabbing the pillows off her bed and starting to hit us.

We screamed so loud. I got a hold of Trent's arm, taking a bite, hearing him scream out, while Olivia and Elijah had it out with the pillows.

"Grandmaaaaa!" Olivia screamed with a laugh just as I hit the ground hard with Trent grabbing my feet, trying to drag me. My shirt rose up to show off my pink panties.

"Let go!" I laughed, trying to kick.

"Say sorry!" he demanded as I kicked some more, with him placing his body on top of mine to keep me still, grabbing my fists. He leaned in so close that those hazel eyes could have burned a hole in my face if they wanted to. Smirking as he stuck his tongue out at me, he attempted to lick me.

"Trent! Let gooo!" I laughed, head whipping back and forth. "I'm not playing with yo' ass! Let go!"

"Say sorry for eating our food," he demanded, tongue moving closer as I laughed.

Before I could admit to anything, a hard knock against the wall immediately stopped the chaos in the room. Looking up, I saw their grandma, who did not play no games, staring hard at all of us.

"All of y'all need to take y'all loud asses to bed now!" she snapped, and Trent quickly got up. I could see their older brother, Shiloh, who was already a junior in high school, smirking hard behind his grandma.

In no time, we were in the room, lights off, laying up in the bed, talking. With the boys' room next door, we could hear the TV on and the light whispers of Elijah and Trent, arguing through the walls.

"What the hell are they doing?" I asked Olivia, looking at her.

"Probably in there watching those nasty porn videos they be stealing from Shiloh," she mumbled, and my eyes lit up.

I sat up in the dark, looking down at my best friend since diaper days. She turned her nose up at me. "What, Taylor?"

"Well, let's go bust they asses then." I laughed. "You saw how they came in here messing with us. Let's go mess with them," I suggested.

"What? Now?" she let out, sitting up.

I nodded before flipping the covers back. We got off the bed and slowly crept to the door, slipping out quietly, and walked down the small hallway. They lived in this old, two-story house in the middle of the straight-up hood on the west side that their grandma had lived in for years. No one really fucked with them because of the last name. The name Carter went a long way in Atlanta. They were like hood royalty, with their dad being the biggest dope dealer back in his day, having an army of niggas doing whatever he needed to be done. I didn't know it was a gang until later on, when Elijah slipped into that lifestyle.

As we got closer to the door, we pressed our ears against the wood, hearing the sounds of a female breathing hard. My eyes nearly fell out of my head as I looked at Olivia, who covered her mouth in a gasp. I took a hairpin from underneath my scarf and started to quietly pick at the lock, knowing they had locked the door. As soon as I heard that click, I glanced at Olivia, who tried so hard not to laugh. After hearing another sound of a female talking, I slowly turned the knob, and bam! We burst right into the room, seeing two boys on the bed, with their tiny dicks out in their hands, eyes wide in horror.

"Get out!" Elijah cried as I laughed, falling to the floor.

"Grandmaaaa!" Trent screamed, trying to pull his jeans up as I looked at the video of a girl having sex with a guy.

"Fuck you calling her for, nigga?" Elijah flipped.

Olivia and I could barely stand up because we were laughing so hard.

Thinking back, I couldn't help but smile to myself as I looked at my wall in my new room. Those were the good times. It was always the good times when you're kids and don't know any better. Now that we were grown, things were different. Sex was no longer a funny joke, but something two adults who were feeling each other did. I had yet to experience it, not because I wanted to be married or whatever. No, I wanted to have sex—like, yesterday—but I couldn't bring myself to be naked in front of a man. I became so scared, so nervous that I just didn't do it. Believe me, I had hella offers, many boyfriends, but the issue was always the same. I don't eat in front of people, and I don't have sex because of body image issues.

Smiling again, I thought about how we had caught them in the act. Hell, I caught Trent trying to have sex with a girl a year after that porn incident. Chuckling, I shook my head, dancing to the beat of the song as I turned around. Without so much as a warning, I glanced up at the figure in the doorway and froze. Trenton Michael Carter. Damn, nigga, he grew into a fine-ass man.

I watched him slowly smile at me, licking his lips as his eyes wandered. Looking him over, I felt the wave of feelings I thought I didn't have for him anymore slowly start to come back. He was tall, still light-bright as ever, with a fit body. I could see his pecs and abs through the white shirt. His face was chiseled to perfection, with those hazel eyes still bright as ever. He had a clean haircut and dressed like he knew he was fine.

I smiled back, realizing I stared a little too long.

"Hi," I mouthed over the music before cutting the song off completely. *Not now, Beyoncé.*

We stared at each other just as a dark-skin guy with dreads popped into my room. My mouth dropped at the sight of Elijah. I mean, I had seen pictures of him online with his music group, but it didn't compare to seeing him in person. He was just as fine.

"Daaaaayuummm! Big Tay!" he screamed while rushing up to me. I wrapped my arms around his neck in laughter, trying to keep his wild self still. "Shawty, look at you! You sexy as fuck! What the fuck happened?"

"Shut up, Elijah." I laughed as he backed up to look me over. Damn. Elijah sneaked up on me. I never thought he would grow into his puppy-dog face, but he looked like a chocolate version of Shiloh with dreads. Tattoos were littering his face and body. "You look good yourself, Carter boy."

"I mean, I know I do, but I can't call you Big Tay no more, shawty," he let out, eyes searching my body hard like I stole something of his. His low-cut eyes locked with mine in curiosity. "You fucking?"

"Nigga!" I laughed, pushing him back. He was always the blunt one, never one to hold back.

I ended up getting caught up talking in the hallway with the other brothers, Talin and Jahiem, about babies on the way for both of them. I didn't get a chance to say much of anything else to Trent, but I guess he was still a little nervous to speak. Maybe I was. I don't know.

The front door opened again, with Ontrell coming in as my mouth dropped. He was the youngest Carter only by three years. I had just turned twenty-four, the triplets would be twenty-four in two weeks, and Trell just turned twenty-one this year. He was the one to always tag along with his big brothers when they all hung out, although everything changed when he came out to his family that he liked boys. He was still very much loved by everyone, minus his dad.

"Oh my God!" I screamed in excitement as he came up to me, hugging me tight. He was looking like he just got his dreads freshly twisted, looking exactly like his brother Anthony with that milky-brown complexion and wide eyes. Never the flamboyant type, always the nicest, he was the one that hung around most of the girls because he was easier to talk to. I don't know if it was because he was younger and we treated him like a baby, or because he was gay. Who knows and who cares?

"Shawty, look at you!" He laughed. "Yo, I remember that day you fought that girl at the playground over Olivia."

"Damn right," I stated proudly. "Can't fuck with my bestie and think I'm going to sit there and watch." As we started talking, bringing up old memories, I couldn't help but glance at Trent from time to time—until he actually glanced back at me, with our eyes locking for a brief second. I looked away quickly, feeling my heart beat a little faster. Moving back to Atlanta might have been a mistake after all.

The Last Lie

Noelle

"So, what's the dick like?" Layla asked, and I nearly coughed up my drink, not expecting the blunt question this early in the day. It was Tuesday, mid-morning. We sat in the local cafeteria at our agency, watching people get in line to order their food. It was colder than usual outside, so I ordered soup and a side salad, feeling dainty and cute in my Michael Kors dress, matching heels, and handbag. I felt fancy. We were waiting on our other coworker, who rarely worked in the building since he did so much outside work with his clients; but every now and then, Tyree would pop in. He was more of a friend to Layla, since I was still getting to know everyone.

Looking around the busy café, taking in the sounds of multiple conversations, I thought about Shiloh and how a place like this would irk him. He was such a loner, preferring his own company. He never liked to be around a lot of people at once, because he said it made him nervous. Nervous for what, I don't know.

"Hey! Noelle!" Layla suddenly let out, snapping her fingers in my face, and I blinked, looking hard at her with wide eyes. "You constantly day-dreaming, girl. You didn't answer my question. What's the sex like?"

"I haven't had sex with him yet." I shrugged, sipping a spoonful of my soup.

Layla let out a gasp, putting her tiny, light hand on her chest. "Bitch, you what?" she questioned, and I laughed. "This nigga is yo' boyfriend and you haven't had sex yet?"

"We just started dating. It's not like it's supposed to happen just like—"

"Uh, if this nigga hasn't asked for any, that means he's getting some from somebody else. Fact!" she stated, and my mouth dropped. "How many boyfriend have you had?"

"One," I admitted softly, thinking about my ex.

"Noelle. Girl!" She laughed, taking a bite out of her fry just as I spotted a familiar body walking toward our café booth. She looked back, seeing Tyree, and immediately went in on me, dragging him into the mix. "Nigga, you need to hurry up and sit down so I can tell you the foolishness Noelle has got going on with this man!"

"Oh Lord," I groaned as Tyree smirked hard at me.

Tyree was the epitome of a gay man. He could be your bestie, a shoulder to cry on, the man you pretend is your boyfriend when you don't want a creep hitting on you at the club. He was all of that in one. He was tall, brown-skin, with a clean-shaved head, small eyes that were filled with attitude, and his lips always pursed, permanently in duck-face. His body was built and toned, and he always dressed like a New Yorker. His fashion sense was out of this world—not better than mine, but he dressed like a well-put man. Like today, he had on a cream-colored trench coach, dark blue jeans, dark brown boots, scarf, and a cute vintage sweater underneath.

"Hey, boo," he said to Layla as he bent down to kiss her cheek. Then he turned to me, smiling hard. "Hey, li'l ho," he said, kissing my cheek as I laughed.

"Why am I the ho?" I shrieked with a smile as he sat down next to me.

"Because I heard about this man you got. How yo' ass just moved here and already got a nigga coming after you?" Tyree started as Layla and I laughed. "I mean, you pretty and all, but damn!"

"Nah-uh, he claiming her. That's her boyfriend now," Layla said as Tyree cocked his head back at me in a dramatic fashion, leaning to the side as he looked me over.

"Oh, okay, bitch. So, we doing it like that?" he pressed as I dropped my head in full-blown shame. "What's his name? What does he look like? What's his zodiac—"

"Nah-uh, get this," Layla continued as I groaned. "So, they haven't had sex yet, and the dude isn't even trying. I told her something ain't right with that."

"Mm-hmm, you want me to check and make sure he's not playing for another team, boo?" Tyree asked.

"I don't think Shiloh is like that," I said more to myself than—

"Wait!" Tyree shrieked, gripping the table as he stared hard at me. "What's his name?"

"Shiloh . . ." I let out slowly, feeling nerves take over. *Is this man gay? I swear on everything I love, I hope—*

"Girl! Shiloh Carter? Please do not tell me you got Shiloh Carter to settle the fuck down with you!" he let out with a laugh.

"His name is Shiloh Carter," I continued, with him still laughing.

"How you know him?" Layla asked greedily as her eyes zoomed in on Tyree, waiting to hear the gossip.

"Girl, that's Trell's older brother! Bitch, we dating brothers!" he stated as I laughed. "I know Shiloh's quiet ass probably a freak too. He'll sneak up on you. Won't say nothing, just do it. I bet he's a nasty nigga in the bed. Mmm," Tyree started, eyes closing as he fantasized about my guy.

"Hey!" I said, hitting his shoulder. "Finish telling me everything you know about him. He rarely opens up to me."

"Well," he started as he leaned in, causing Layla and I to lean in as well, "he's quiet as hell, as you already know. When I'm with Trell and his brothers, he'll speak when he wants to. Even if someone asks him a question, rarely will the nigga answer it. I've seen him run through girls like water, but never has he had a girlfriend. I don't know if it's something with you to make him want to settle down, but you are the first girl I know that's he's considering a girlfriend— if that's true in itself. A lot of females try and claim that nigga, but he's quick to shut it down. So, how you know y'all really together?" he questioned. I sat back in my chair, thinking hard. "Just because that nigga take you out to eat don't mean shit. Girl, when I tell you he don't do that relationship shit, he really don't. Prefers to be alone. But if you are? Bitch, we double dating!"

"So, why isn't he trying to push for sex?" I questioned out of curiosity. Normally, I was not the type to talk about my personal life, but Shiloh really left me no choice.

"I mean, maybe he don't want it." Tyree shrugged, already texting on his phone. "I gotta call my boo and tell him."

"I think he's fucking somebody else," Layla let out, and Tyree pursed his lips out at her with a roll of his eyes.

"Bitch, you stay looking for drama where there is none. One day a bitch is going to whoop yo' ass over that bullshit. Keep talking and it might be Noelle," Tyree said.

I laughed, waving him off.

So, I couldn't even make it through the lunch without asking all these questions and questioning everything about Shiloh and me. Even though we texted back and forth occasionally throughout the day, I still wondered what we really were. The sex thing, I was kind of grateful, because I'm a virgin. There! I said it. It's out there in this book for you guys to soak up. I'm a virgin. I was told to wait until I was married to give it up. Didn't think I could wait until marriage, but I was definitely waiting for the right man and right time, because I pictured my first time being romantic.

So, with that being said, I didn't get a chance to tell anyone that Shiloh was picking me up since my car would be in the shop all week. I didn't want to tell anyone either, because I didn't want any attention drawn to me—not with Layla, and definitely not with Tyree. Yet, as I was staring at my reflection in the mirror later in the bathroom, Layla was right there next to me, yacking away with her mouth.

"So, anyway, I told the nigga, if we not working toward being something more, then ain't no reason to talk again," she continued.

"So, what happened?" I asked as I brushed out my dark, straightened hair.

"I ended up sleeping with him again." She sighed as I looked at her short frame, shaking my head. "I can't help it. The sex is good," she said, shrugging.

As she continued to talk, I looked myself over in the all-black ensemble: black Michael Kors long-sleeve dress with a skinny belt around the waist, black Michael Kors heels, and a matching tote bag. My cute silver watch matched the silver in the shoes and bag and silver-studded pearl earrings. My hair was pulled into a high

bun, with a swoop barely covering my left eye.
My dark complexion was flawless, with light lip-
stick and eye makeup. Know that every time you
read about me, I stay dressed to kill. It's my profession, and I expect nothing less of myself.

Feeling my phone vibrate in my bag, I quickly
grabbed it, seeing a message from Shiloh, saying he was outside. *Damn it, Layla, go home
already.* I did not want her to see this man pick
me up.

"So anyway," she continued as we walked out
of the bathroom, passing another woman who
was on her way in. "I suggest you make sure
that nigga isn't fucking with another chick and
just keeping you around because you live next
door."

"I don't think he's doing that," I mumbled,
getting on the elevator.

"How do you know, Noelle?" she pressed as I
fought the urge to roll my eyes. She was a short
little thing with a lot of mouth, I swear. "I mean,
this nigga seems like he's only hitting you up at
night anyway. What the fuck else y'all do besides
chill on the couch in the middle of the night
and—"

"Layla, I don't know what this man's inten-
tions are. We barely been together a week. It's all
still new," I said, cutting her off in exasperation
as we came out on the first floor.

Walking toward the glass revolving doors as I put on my Michael Kors coat, I spotted his black Mustang sitting right outside in the no parking zone. All the windows were tinted, so I couldn't see his face.

"All I'm saying is be careful. He looks like he sly as shit, probably running game on you now and you don't even know it. This is Atlanta, boo, not the little country town that you came from," she said, following behind me as we stepped out into the cold city air. "He probably don't even—"

She finally stopped talking when the car door opened and Shiloh stepped out slowly, looking down the street at the traffic before resting his eyes on me—no smile, no anything, just looking.

"Damn," Layla mumbled as I smirked, walking down the steps, grabbing on to the gold rail. He licked his lips as I looked him over like he was doing me. He stood tall in his black coat, wearing his camouflage pants, black boots, black long-sleeve top with the tiny green Polo logo in the corner, and thick black coat with fur on the hood, looking like winter in New York. His dark, curly hair was shining, with those dark pink lips against his almost vanilla-like complexion. Those eyes, though . . . Those naturally sleepy bedroom eyes always did it for me.

Walking toward him as the wind whipped by, I hugged him. His hand slid around my waist inside the coat, sitting just a few seconds over the booty. Yeah, I said seconds. No other way to describe the placement of his hand.

"You look good," he said softly against my ear as I smiled, getting a good smell of him. He always smelled good. It's the biggest turn-on when a man smells fresh and clean.

I pulled back, waving to Layla, who kept her eyes hard on Shiloh before walking around the car to get inside. As soon as I got inside, I started telling him about my day, not even caring whether he wanted to listen. The only time he stopped me was to tell me he needed to go to the grocery store to pick up something to eat for tonight. Yet, he kept driving in stop-and-go traffic, one hand on the steering wheel, weaving in and out of lanes before we eventually made it to a Publix. It was my favorite store.

We stepped out into the cold evening air as we walked briskly to the store, my heels clicking against the pavement, his keys jingling in his hand as he slipped them into his pocket.

"What are you cooking tonight?" I asked as he looked back at me with a smirk, grabbing a shopping cart. "What's so funny?"

"I'm buying some food so you can cook for me," he said softly as he pushed the cart inside the store with me laughing.

"You didn't even ask!" I shrieked, following behind him with a huge grin. "How do you know I don't have plans to step out tonight?"

"Because you're going to be with me," he stated, no hesitation in his voice whatsoever. I just smiled as he looked back at me, both hands gripping the cart. "I want something heavy. Something to sit on my stomach for a while."

"Like pasta?" I pressed, thinking about all the different types of pasta that I could make.

"I'm not picky," he stated, looking at the different assortments of food on the shelves.

Looking at him, I thought about the conversation we'd had at work during lunch, wondering, curious. I decided to test the waters. As soon as a couple walked past us, I went in.

"Can I ask a question?" I asked nervously, and he looked at me, eyes wide. I know he probably felt like I was about to invade his privacy, but I had to know. "Why don't you . . . or why haven't you—" I looked around anxiously to make sure

no one was listening. I almost felt like Layla
would pop up any minute to ask for me.

"Why don't I what?" he asked, looking hard at
me.

"Ask me to have sex, or try me in a sexual way,"
I mumbled. I watched his face slowly turn from
stone cold to a sudden burst of laughter as he
gripped his stomach.

"Shawty, what?" He laughed, grabbing onto
the cart like I had said the funniest shit in the
world. Now I was offended. It was an honest
question that deserved an honest answer.

"I'm serious, Shiloh!"

"Noelle," he said with a shake of his head as
he tried to pull himself together, like I'd said the
best joke in the world. "Baby, who the fuck you
got in yo' head right now?"

"What does that mean?"

"It means who all in yo' ear? Who got you
asking that bullshit? I know we still getting
to know each other, but I got you figured out
already, and I know that's not you. So, who's the
female that's in yo' ear? That short, light-skin
bitch who be staring at a nigga like she want it?"
he questioned as my mouth dropped. One, I'd
never heard him talk this much since . . . never.
Two, was he talking about Layla?

"Nobody is in my ear, Shiloh. It was my question," I started, clearly upset as I pushed the

shopping cart to keep moving. He followed behind me, still laughing. "And you don't have me figured out."

"Yeah, I do." He smirked. "You a good girl, sweetheart, spoiled by her daddy. Used to having things her way. Probably the only child, and probably used to other chicks hating on you, so you put on that fake smile and keep it moving. Don't smoke, barely drink, and never had sex before—"

"What?" I shrieked as I turned around, seeing him grin. I didn't know whether to cuss him out or enjoy his mouth actually forming a smile. It was rare, yet it worked for him. He should do it more often. "You think I'm a virgin?" I pressed. So, he had me figured out for the most part. Yet, I couldn't let him have it all.

"I know you are. I can look at you and tell you never been with a man on that level before. You probably had niggas coming at you like crazy because you're beautiful as fuck, but never on that level, shawty," he stated with a knowing smirk. "Right?"

"Wrong," I retorted, matching his smirk with my own before his face dropped. "I had sex before. I just don't do it often," I lied, pushing the cart past him.

"You lying," he continued.

I shook my head, looking back at him, biting my lower lip with a flirty wink before I kept moving. Let me just say for the readers, that's as far as my sex appeal goes. I can flirt, but that's it. He read me like a book, and I didn't like that. I felt like reading him was like reading a book with a language in it that has yet to be discovered.

"If you say so." I shrugged in a cute manner as he came to stand beside me. I started grabbing things to make some basic Alfredo pasta with baked chicken on the side. I could hear him snickering to himself as he continued to stare at me, watching me look over food before finally, I stared back. I was holding two packages of raw chicken in my hand.

"What, Shiloh?" I pressed as he smiled.

"You're not a virgin?" he repeated.

I shook my head no.

"Okay," he said, nodding. "We're going to test that out tonight. I'm going to see how far you let me get before you decide to tell the truth."

"Do what you think you gotta do, big guy," I mumbled, eyeing the meat.

Oh Lord, what am I even starting? What have I caused? Yet, I couldn't back down now. I was already in too deep. Way too deep.

"Let this be the first and only time you lie to me, Noelle," he said in a serious voice as

I looked at him, rolled my eyes, and kept moving.

"What do you want to drink?" I asked as we strolled through the grocery store. Grabbing a few things, I wanted to make it a full meal with desserts. We were standing in the frozen goods section. I was looking at the cheesecakes as Shiloh patiently waited for me to make a decision, leaning on the front of the cart, eyes on me.

I read the back of a few frozen goods, not even realizing a guy had walked up next to me, smiling hard. He was some chubby, light-skin guy who looked like he had a fetish for dark-skin girls as he looked me up and down. His friends were waiting for him farther down the aisle, watching as he licked his thick lips at me.

"What's yo' name, sexy?" he asked boldly as he leaned on the glass door, eyes everywhere but my face. It was pure disrespect. If I felt it, I knew Shiloh felt it.

"I—"

"Her name is 'mothafucka, I know you see me standing right here,'" Shiloh cut in, still leaning on the cart, cutting his eyes hard at the man. The guy looked at Shiloh, looked back at his friends, before looking at me again. Unbelievable.

"You heard him," I said, not even glancing at the guy as I grabbed a cheesecake, handing it to Shiloh. If there was one thing I didn't tolerate, it was disrespectful BS like that. "My name is 'mothafucka, I know you see him standing right there,'" I repeated, and the guy cocked his head back.

"Shit. Whatever then," the guy mumbled with a smack of his teeth, walking back to his flock.

"These young niggas gonna get popped one day if they not careful," Shiloh mumbled as he pushed the cart, smirking at me. "You ready?"

"Why are you smiling?"

"First it's why I don't say nothing, why do I always stare at you, why I haven't made a move on you yet. Why this, why that? Why you got so many questions for me?"

"Because," I said, following beside him as we headed to checkout. "I can't figure you out."

"And you never will," he concluded.

As soon as we got to my place, I started in the kitchen, letting the water boil a little before I put the noodles in. Chicken was in the oven, and Shiloh sat in the living room, already making himself comfortable, popping a movie in.

"I'm going to change," I told him as I walked toward my room.

"Aye, I haven't forgotten you were supposed to prove me right," he stated, and I stopped dead in my tracks to stare at him, smiling.

"Shiloh, I'm not a virgin. We can do this now if you really feel like you have to prove this big point that you think I'm lying to you," I snapped. I knew I was talking out of my ass, but I had a competitive side of me that didn't want to back down.

He just smirked at me. "How long you gonna keep this shit up, Noelle? Like, real talk?"

"Whatever, Shiloh," I said, waving him off as I went into the room, closing the door with a lock, just in case he did try something. I slipped out of my dress and slipped into the closet, which led to my bathroom, and took a quick shower. Once I was done, I put on a T-shirt and some shorts, with cute fuzzy socks. I looked at myself in the mirror, smiling. My hair was still wet, nipples piercing through the shirt, and my body smelled like honey and shea butter.

I walked out, seeing he was laid up on the couch, shirt off, camouflage pants sagging, showing off his black boxer briefs as he looked at me.

"You trying the fuck out of me right now." Shiloh laughed slowly as his eyes went back to the TV.

"You trying yourself," I mumbled, walking into the living room. I sat down on the couch next to him as his eyes shifted toward me, sitting low, wandering over my body.

"So, you still keeping this lie up?" he questioned as I threw my hands up in exasperation.

"I'm not lying!" I lied with a laugh. "I've had plenty of sex before, Shiloh. I know how to throw it back and all."

He stared at me, nodding slowly as he reached for the remote to cut the TV off. It was pitch black outside as silence took over the small house. He was about to try it.

Oh my God, I'd talked enough shit. Now it was time to talk myself out of it. Before I could even open my mouth, he stood up, pulling his pants up as his toned, tatted, light-caramel body flexed with each movement. I quickly stood up, already seeing the look in his eyes. I wasn't ready for this.

"Wait, you—"

"I what?" he started, moving closer to me. I kept backing up, heart beating like crazy as he grabbed me by the waist, picked me up in one easy move, and walked toward my room, eyes never leaving mine. "You scared?" he pressed with a smirk.

"No, I just don't think it should be like—"

"Not how you imagined your first time?" he asked, pushing the door open to the dark room with his foot. I said nothing. He closed the door, causing it to be completely pitch black as my mouth went dry. I wasn't ready. God knows I wasn't ready for this. Would it be painful? Would I bleed? I felt the covers hit my back as he laid me down, laying on top of me gently. I could see him smiling hard as he hovered over me in the dark.

"You still not trying to tell me you a virgin?" he asked.

I shook my head no. *Ugh! What the fuck is wrong with me? Maybe I'm curious. Maybe I want to know what it feels like. I could be ready for him, right?* All these thoughts running through my head came to a stop when I felt his lips touch my neck ever so gently. I felt the chills go throughout my body as he continued, taking his sweet time like we had all night.

"You still gonna keep lying to me?" he asked in a low voice. Both of his hands slid up underneath my shirt, and I heard him groan in response as he exposed my breasts, eyeing them like he was debating which to take first.

The moment he made up his mind, I arched into him, a moan escaping my mouth as he took his time, wet mouth covering the nipple. There was a stretch of thin saliva in between when he pulled back, eyeing the nipple in hunger before widening his mouth to take it all in again. His tongue curled against the sensitive nub.

Jesus . . . Jesus . . . Lord, what is going on right now? I could barely manage his mouth, let alone the rest of him. Gripping his shoulders, I felt him pull at my shorts before sitting up to pull them off completely, revealing naked flesh.

"You not going to tell me to stop?" Shiloh asked, kissing my stomach. He looked up at me as I looked down at him, watching him spread my legs wider before standing up to take his pants off. His . . . thing was bursting through the briefs as he came back down in between me.

"Shiloh," I whispered as he came up to kiss me on the lips. Just like that, I felt like I had a boost of courage, wrapping my arms around his neck as I deepened the kiss, taking full control. Maybe I could do this. It was just sex, after all. I mean, girls fight men over things like this, but it couldn't be all that good to cause drama. Just sex, nothing more.

I started going for his neck, biting down before kissing that same spot, hearing him groan. His body tightened up so quick that I almost thought something was wrong.

"Shit, fuck is you doing?" He moaned as I smiled, continuing my attack on his neck. So, we had matching hot spots.

Feeling brave, I reached down and grabbed his dick, slipping my hand in his boxer briefs with a strong grip.

"You not ready for that," he breathed, trying to move my hand away, but I kept still. "Yo, I'm serious, Noelle."

"So am I," I stated, slipping his shorts off as he kicked himself out of them. We were both naked where it counts.

Feeling him lay in between me, I suddenly realized just how close I was to losing my virginity. I wasn't ready. No, no, no, no! I wasn't ready!

"Noelle," he breathed, gripping my thighs in each hand, lifting me up slightly before spreading my legs wider.

"Huh?" I let out, feeling him lay back down, kissing the side of my mouth, hand running through my wet hair.

"Baby, tell me the truth. I'm at the point where I can't . . ." His words trailed off as I shifted a little, causing the tip to hit right at the entrance, wet and ready. I didn't mean for that to happen. His head dropped in defeat. He took in a deep breath through his nose. Silence ˙. . . tense silence . . .

"Shiloh, I—" I stopped immediately when I felt him trying to push himself in, and without so much as a thought, I let out in panic, "Please don't hurt me."

He froze in mid-movement, looking at me. I couldn't see his face, but I knew his low eyes were on me, gazing hard in the darkness.

"I'm a virgin. You were right," I mumbled.

He leaned in and kissed me on the lips before standing up to put his pants back on. I reached for my shorts, putting them back on as he lay down on the bed next to me. I popped the lamp light on, seeing his eyes were closed, hand on his balls, face muscles twitching in hard thought.

"Shiloh?" I called out. He said nothing. I didn't know if he was upset, irritated, or what. He almost looked like he was in pain. "Shiloh?" He opened his eyes, giving me the side-eye look. "I'm sorry?" He closed his eyes again, wincing like he was in pain as his grip tightened on himself before loosening up. "I don't know when I'll be ready for sex," I concluded, knowing this was when guys usually took the chance to leave after that statement.

"I'll wait on you," was all he said, and I smiled. It was the first time a guy had ever said that to me and meant it.

"Thank you," I said, kissing his cheek affectionately.

He let out a deep, heavy sigh. "Let this be the first and only lie you tell me, Noelle," he repeated, one eye open as he looked at me. I just nodded.

Movie Night

Tia

Looking at myself in the bathroom mirror, I stared at the reflection of my stomach. I couldn't believe I was fucking pregnant and starting to show. It was going on eight weeks, last week of October. I barely got a chance to see Jahiem, but tonight was supposed to be our very first official date as a couple, Friday night at Atlantic Station, for a simple movie. My friends thought we were cute together, but honestly? The nigga and I stayed arguing over dumb shit. We barely lasted five minutes on the phone without arguing. Like, last night, it was 2 a.m. over here, and I couldn't sleep because I didn't feel good. He was over on the West Coast with his brothers doing a studio session for another artist when he called me.

"Hello?" I answered, turning the TV down as I put my bag of Skittles on the nightstand, keeping a few in my hand to pop in my mouth.

I could hear the chaos of his brothers in the background and the sound of a female voice.

"Nah, bruh, chill out." Jahiem laughed. "She not dancing without money. That's how all females are."

"Uh, nigga, you called me?" I snapped, pulling the covers up to my neck.

"Yeah, why the fuck you still up?"

"Because—" I stopped in mid sentence as he laughed at something someone else said before turning his attention to the female. I could barely make out what she was saying, but I knew the bitch was speaking to him, and I knew I didn't like that shit, regardless of who she was. "Fuck it," I let out before hanging up. My stomach was in all kinds of knots, I had a headache, and I felt bloated like fuck. I didn't need this aggravating shit happening to me right now. Of course, he called me back, and that started up a whole new argument that I didn't feel like having.

"So, you hanging up on a nigga now?" he asked with a laugh. "Yo, this is why I don't fuck with young bitches, man. Y'all on that childish shit."

"So go fuck with a old ho then, bruh. Miss me with that. You called me, but having side conversations while I'm on the phone. I don't feel good, I'm tired but can't sleep, and I'm irritated that you wasting my time."

"You done?" he asked, and I heard a door close. "You done bitching?"

"Jahiem." I sighed, closing my eyes. "Nigga, what the fuck do you want?"

"See, this why I don't talk to you. This is why we not going to fucking make it, because you so fucking negative, and that attitude got a nigga ready to check the fuck out of you every time you open yo' mouth."

"I wish you would," I mumbled, cutting the TV off altogether as I lay there in the dark. I let out a cough before sneezing, sniffing up the remains. Fuck, I just wanted to sleep without feeling my stomach turn.

"You ain't gotta wish for that shit," he muttered back, and I rolled my eyes. I wasn't even going to respond to him. "What you doing, though?"

"Laying in the bed," I sniffed. "Feeling like shit."

"You got the heat on? You like sleeping in a fucking ice storm."

"I sleep better when it's cold," I argued, hearing him smack his teeth.

"Go cut the heat on, Tiana," he demanded. "Get up and go cut that shit on."

"So I can be sweating all night? Uh, no. I just straightened out my hair, nigga," I told him, patting my tightly wrapped scarf. Since I knew

I was seeing him the next day, I didn't want to hear him bitch about me wearing a weave or heavy makeup.

"Go cut that shit on," he pressed, and I groaned with a smack of my teeth. Nigga was relentless. For the sake of this conversation, I lied and told him I cut it on.

"You looked at the website I told you about?"

"Yeah, I saw it," I told him as we slipped into a conversation about the pregnancy. Just like that, our bipolar asses were on some calm shit. It never failed.

Now, present day, Friday night, he was in town for the weekend, and I planned on surprising him with my look. As you know, I love my makeup and my eyelashes and eyebrows being filled in, my long weave, and my bougie, stank attitude that could drive a nigga crazy. Tonight, I was going to try something different.

Looking at myself in the mirror, I smoothed my dark brown hair down, loving the feel of it. Underneath the weave, I was natural all the way. I just wasn't the type to rock an afro. Some bitches can pull it off, but I wasn't into that sister-soul look all the damn time. Yet, I was dating a nigga who was low-key Black Panther'd out, so I wanted to appeal to his eyes by keeping it simple, wearing some cute acid wash high-waist jeans and a cream-colored sweater with caramel-colored riding boots. I had gold hoops in my ears, with my dark brown hair falling just to my shoulders with a cute side bang. Bitch, I was cute, and what? You couldn't tell me shit right now that I didn't already know.

My girl Porscha was out with her side boo, my roommate Jade was with Trent most nights, and I hadn't heard from or seen Jordyn since I beat her ass. Now, the more I thought about it, the more I wished I could take it back, because the only reason I fucked her up was that she was with Elijah and I wasn't. If that shit was true about them being together, the last thing I needed was Jahiem finding out that I was fucking hoes up over his younger brother.

Suddenly, I heard a knock on the main door, and I smiled. Jahiem Carter. I couldn't believe I was getting excited over this nigga. Never would I have guessed he would be the one I was falling for, but as I opened the door, I felt like my panties just dropped at the sight of him. Nigga stayed growing facial hair. As soon as he cut it off, it was there the next damn day. He was standing tall, with those wide, thick shoulders, wearing a long-sleeve black Polo button-up shirt bouncing off his light complexion, black straight-leg pants showing me the print of his dick that I knew all

too well, and matching Gucci shoes. Nigga wore
a black blazer jacket, trying to stunt on someone
with a simple chain around his neck, and a
trimmed goatee, with that foolish grin on his
face. All of those Carter boys were pretty niggas.
It wasn't just Trent, and it definitely wasn't a
light-skin thing, because Elijah was as much of a
pretty boy as Trent, if not more.

"Nigga, what the fuck is going on here?" I
asked, poking his dick print. He looked down
before smiling. Shit was pressing hard against
the jeans.

"You look nice." He smiled, eyes roaming.
"That's yo' hair?"

"Yep."

He smiled even harder before stepping closer
to me, coming in for a hug. I didn't realize how
much I had missed this nigga until I was in
his arms, smelling him, feeling him, and just
being with him. We hadn't seen each other since
homecoming weekend, and that was two weeks
ago.

"Can we go get something to eat? I'm starving,"
I let out, letting go of him as I quickly grabbed
my purse and coat.

Of course the car ride to a simple restaurant
was anything but enjoyable. The entire ride, we
argued over petty shit. No, let me take that back.

It wasn't petty, because I went through this nigga's phone, seeing he was texting another ho, sending dick pics her way while she sent ass shots his way. I got one better for you, readers. She wasn't the only bitch in his phone he was fucking with while he was out of town. Tiana will never be made a fool of. Let's get that straightened out first.

"So you think—" I continued, hearing him groan as he focused on driving. We were stuck in traffic on the highway, late Friday night, just trying to get to midtown. "Nigga, don't fucking groan like you not trying to hear what the fuck I got to say! Why try and start a relationship with me if you still trying to continue to have yo' fucking single life? That doesn't make sense to me."

"I don't know, Tia," he said in a dry tone, looking out his window.

"Nah, nigga, you know," I said, scrolling through his phone, reading the text messages. When he tried reaching for his phone for a third time, I slapped his hand out of the way. "Move! Let me see what the fuck else you sticking yo' dick into besides me."

"You on some other shit man, I swear." He laughed sarcastically. "I told you I'm not fucking with none of these girls. We talk and shit, but it's nothing more than that."

"Mm-hmm," I mumbled, reading an incoming text. I was that kind of girlfriend. Fuck what y'all think. I'll go through yo' phone, yo' IG, Facebook, yo' fucking life, nigga. I'm in it.

Suddenly, out of nowhere, he reached down in my bag and took my phone while I was screaming at him, trying to take it back.

"Nah! Move! You want to go through my shit, then let me go through yours!" he snapped as my heart started to beat uncontrollably. I had some shit in there I know he wasn't trying to see, like the conversation with Porscha and me talking about Trent possibly being the father of this baby.

"Take yo' fucking phone then, nigga!" I snapped, throwing it hard at him as he blocked his face with his arm held up while scrolling through my IG. "Jahiem, give me my phone."

"Who the fuck is IGETMONEYBANDZ21?" he pressed. "This nigga sending you dick pics on yo' DM, and you responding to that shit. Oh, but look at this shit!" he yelled sarcastically as he continued to read out my private conversations between me and a couple of guys.

"I swear I will get out this car and walk back home if you don't give me my phone back, Jahiem!" I threatened, hand on the door handle. We were in the far left lane, not moving a damn inch but every so often. and he snorted.

"Get the fuck on out then," he stated, going through my Facebook messages. "Shit, I knew you was a ho, but you pregnant, and still acting like you single with no kids. Look at this shit! You talking about how you can suck a nigga's dick on Facebook."

"Jahiem," I said in a low voice, letting him know how serious I was. "I swear if you don't give me the damn phone—"

"Get the fuck on out, but you not getting this phone back until I go through this shit like you just did me," he said. "Don't slam my door on yo' way out, either."

Looking at him, seeing him reading a conversation between my ex and me out loud, I couldn't help myself. On Facebook, I knew there were old messages between Trent and me talking about hooking up. I couldn't let him see that shit, so I hauled off on his ass, mushing him hard in the face, trying to grab my phone.

"Give me my phone back!" I screamed, hitting him hard.

"Yo, sit yo' wild ass back in the seat!" he yelled, trying to block my hands from his face, still holding a tight grip on my phone. All you could see in the car was two people looking like they were slap-boxing each other. I knew other drivers were looking at us like we had lost our damn minds in the middle of this Atlanta night traffic. "Hit me again!" he threatened, voice becoming hard as he stared at me, daring me.

"Nigga, you ain't about to do shit," I retorted, mushing him hard in the face, making his head jerk back. Without warning, he pushed me back in the seat so hard, nearly slamming my body against the door. My eyes grew wide at his actions as I stared at him.

"You keep fucking trying a nigga, you gon' get fucking tried back! I said stop putting yo' hands on me, did I not?"

I just stared at him, seeing the rage in his eyes subside as he threw the phone at me, slamming it hard into my lap. "I don't give a fuck about who you texting and who you talking to on the side. All I was trying to do was prove to you that you not as innocent like you trying to come off. Don't call me out on my shit if you not ready to get the same in return. Don't put yo' hands on me if you not ready to get hands put on you. Understand?" he yelled.

I said nothing; just looked at my phone, cutting it off, trying to hold back tears. We sat in silence as the traffic continued, trying to lighten up on the highway.

"Fuck you got me acting outside of myself," he mumbled, turning the radio on. "You can sit there like a child on that quiet game shit. I don't give a fuck. You like attention, you like shit being yo' way, and you used to fucking with li'l boys who play into that shit. I'm going to tell you now so you know from now own, I'm a grown-ass man. My name is Jahiem Deshaun Carter. I'm not buying yo' shit, because I see right through it. I fucked with bitches like you before. I know the game, shawty, and I'm not playing it with you. So, tell me now. I can turn around and take you the fuck home, or you can get yo' shit together, act like a fucking woman with sense, and we can get something to eat and watch this movie. Yo' choice," he said, looking over at me.

I wiped my eyes, feeling stupid, like a child being chastised by her daddy. "We can eat," I mumbled, clearing my throat as I took out my small compact mirror, checking my face. My eyes were red from filling up with petty tears.

The rest of the ride was silent, except for him getting on the phone, talking to one of his brothers. We decided at the last minute to just head straight to the movie theater and eat there. Of course, Halloween was the best time to see a scary movie. We still didn't speak a word to each other because he was still mad, and I was too, yet the nigga had the nerve to bitch about seeing a scary movie. *After you did all that fussing in*

*the car, trying to look like big shit, you scared
to see a movie?*

"Why you trying to see this shit?" he started as
we walked down the packed hallway, looking for
the movie show times up above.

"You don't have to watch it, Jahiem," I said
quietly, heading toward the door on the left
with my popcorn and Milk Duds in hand. He
held on to our red Slushies, face looking twisted
in irritation. "There are plenty of other movies
showing. You don't have to watch this with me,
but I want to see it, so hand me my drink," I told
him with my hand out.

He dropped his head and pushed open the
wooden door leading into the dark theater with
the previews already showing. As soon as we
found some good seats, I could hear him groan
in irritation once more. *Yet, I'm the childish one?
Okay. Bet.* I just ignored him, setting my purse
on his lap as I held onto the food, munching
away.

Now, let me tell y'all, I tried my hardest to stay
mad at this nigga, but he made it too easy for me
to laugh at him. He was terrified of scary movies.
I mean, I glanced over at him from time to time,
seeing he either didn't look at the screen, or I
would catch him out the side of my eye, jumping
in his seat.

"I can't handle this shit, bruh," he mumbled, looking around like he was trying to find the nearest escape. "The fucking music, the dumb shit white people do; I can't watch this," he complained as someone from behind shhh'd him. He immediately turned around. "Nigga, who the fuck you telling to be quiet?"

"Jahiem—"

"We're trying to watch the movie," the white guy snapped.

"So watch the fucking movie then, bruh! That don't have shit to do with—"

"Jahiem!" I let out, gripping his chin so he could face forward. In an attempt to get him to be quiet, a girl in front of me turned around, glaring hard at me. "Bitch, who the fuck are you looking at? Not me."

"You need to be quiet."

"You need to turn the fuck around before I—"

"Shhhh!" another said.

"How about all of y'all shut the fuck up?" Jahiem yelled out loud, starting an all-out verbal war, us against everyone else, with us being the only black people.

Someone yelled out, "Go back to Africa!"

I told his ass we should have went to Atlantic Station, I thought as I was going off on the bitch in front of me, while Jahiem had the row behind us, straight going in. There were a few that tried to calm everyone down by being the peacemakers, but when I felt a cup hit the back of my head, I turned around quick, seeing three white guys and three girls laughing. Regardless of whether the shit was empty or not, they tried it.

"So, we throwing shit now?!" I screamed, throwing my box of Milk Duds at them, missing like hell. Jahiem turned his attention quick to me, already trying to figure out what was happening.

"Who did it?" he questioned, taking his jacket off. We could hear the group laughing like the shit was funny.

"What the fuck you gonna do about it?" one said as I started walking over seats, with Jahiem grabbing me.

"Hold up, baby. Lemme get 'em," he started as the lights cut on. The movie was still going, but nobody was watching that shit.

"I'll show you what the fuck I'm going to do about it!" I screamed, smacking Jahiem's hand out of the way as we both headed toward the group, not caring if security was on the way.

"Oh my God, she's so ghetto." One of the girls laughed just as I made it to the row in front of theirs. You could tell they were all talk and no bite, because the bitch got scared seeing I was an arm's length away from her.

"I'm what?" I questioned, hands on my hips as the three girls backed up. "You called me ghetto? Bitch, I'll show you ghetto. Throw something at me again!"

"I didn't even do it!" one girl yelled, trying to back away with Jahiem coming at them from the aisle.

"Who threw that shit at my girl? Which one of y'all coon mothafuckas did that shit?"

"Speak up!" I snapped, seeing the white boys react to the word *coon*. One of them didn't take it too lightly, and he stepped to Jahiem, who was twice his size.

"Oh, you can call me a coon, but if I call you all a nigger, it's a fucking race—"

Jahiem, without so much as a slight hesitation, hit the shit out of ol' boy, while I reached for Becky 1 and Becky 2's blond hair, yanking them down over the seats. I could hear screams and calls for security and police as Jahiem handled two white boys, with another running for help.

These girls weren't about that fighting life. They made that shit too easy for me, so after fucking them up one good time, I hopped over the seat and went for the lanky white boy who was trying to help his friend against Jahiem. Jumping on his back, I went for that neck, trying to choke the fuck out of him, gripping his stringy hair. Yeah, I'm that crazy. You ain't gotta tell me. Jahiem damn near stomped ol' boy into the fucking floor before coming at dude, hitting him, blow after blow in the face and stomach.

Everything was happening so fast, with people trying to break it up. It wasn't over until the police came, grabbing Jahiem like a common criminal and slamming him to the ground with his hands behind his back, shouting out orders. I felt my arm get yanked as officers came at me, pulling me off the white boy, who had people trying to help him while we were getting handcuffed. Bullshit. Straight bullshit.

"You need to arrest those mothafuckas!" Jahiem yelled, face mushed in the carpet. "I didn't do shit nobody else wouldn't have done!"

Watching Jahiem get handled by the cops had me heated to the point where I felt myself trying to resist against the ones handling me. "Nigga, let go of me!" I screamed, yanking away from them just as one grabbed the back of my head and slammed me hard into the ground, face first, while jamming a knee on my back, causing me to cry out in pain.

Jahiem's eyes lit up, watching in horror as he saw how the cops handled me.

"Aye, get the fuck off of her!" Jahiem demanded. "She didn't do shit!"

I could feel the tears coming down as I looked at Jahiem, both of us laid on this nasty-ass carpet with everyone watching. Cops were saying something to us, but we only had eyes for each other as the cold metal clinked hard around my wrists.

"You good, mama?" he asked in a low voice, despite all the chaos going on around us, with people telling their side of the story to the officers and security guards. I nodded, knowing I probably looked a hot mess.

"Are you?" I asked, watching them lift him up to stand on his own two feet before grabbing me to stand up.

"I'm good if you are," was all he said as we were both escorted out of the theater.

Tyree

"Shit," I mumbled as I crept up to my door. It was Friday night, going on two o'clock in the morning, and I was just now getting home from a night with my ex-boyfriend. So, as you know, I was supposed to get back at Ontrell for fucking around on me. I was going to sleep with my ex and enjoy it. Yet, I couldn't bring myself to do it. We went out to eat, hung out a bit just to catch up, and that was it. He tried it, though. I mean, who wouldn't? I just didn't have it in me to step outside of my relationship. I loved Trell too much to do that, but it made me realize he didn't love me back. How can someone cheat on you constantly, sleep with other people, only to come home to you and, with a straight face, say he loves you? It didn't make sense to me. It opened my eyes to a lot of bullshit I didn't want to believe.

Fumbling with my keys in the lock, I finally got the door open and saw the lights were on in my room and music was playing. So, he was actually home before me. That would be a first. I stepped inside with my UGG boots, slipping those off at the door just as Ontrell stepped out of the doorway to our bedroom, hands gripping the top of the door. He was shirtless, with his locs down, wearing plaid pajama bottoms, looking oh so fine; but I could feel my heart was permanently worn out with him. I didn't feel the same way after being with my ex. Ontrell Carter couldn't possibly love me like he said he did.

"Where you been at?" he questioned in a serious voice. "I called ol' girl to see if you was still working, and she said she hasn't spoken to you all day."

"Since when do you care, nigga?" I mumbled, moving past him to get to my room. I took my coat off, sitting down on the bed as he walked in, looking hard at me like he was ready to start a fight.

"What the fuck is yo' problem now, Ty? I'm here for the fucking weekend to spend time with you. I'm not out there fucking nobody else. I'm here at this house by myself, waiting on you, and you strolling in like you about that life. So, I'm going to ask you again: where the fuck you been at, nigga?"

I just looked at the man I fell in love with two years ago. I gave him two years of my time; two years I couldn't get back if I tried. To hear him complain about being here alone, waiting up for me, was almost funny. That's all I did, night after night.

"I just needed some time to think about us," I said quietly.

"Oh, yeah? What did you come up with?" he pressed sarcastically, leaning up against the wall, arms folded across his chest. "What the fuck is wrong with you? Why you so quiet? Usually I can't get you to shut the fuck up with yo' nagging."

I just stared at Ontrell, feeling my eyes water. "I want to break up," I said, and his eyes grew wide, arms falling to his side. "I don't want to live with you anymore. I don't want shit to do with you after this, and I want you to lose my fucking number. I'm done," I said, wiping my eyes as the tears came down. It had to be done. My heart, my chest felt so heavy, so full that I could barely breathe.

"You're not serious, Tyree," he snorted as I got up, going through my phone.

The first person that came to mind was Noelle. Although I was still getting to know her, she was the only girl that knew what it was like fucking with these damn Carter boys. I didn't want to sleep in my own fucking house no more. Just the sight of Ontrell made me think about me sleeping with Eric and how I couldn't do it because I was so in love with Trell. That's how it should be. You shouldn't be in a relationship if you can so easily step out with someone else.

Grabbing a bag, I started to pack some clothes, hearing Trell go off, bashing me in the process like he always did.

"You not going no-fucking-where! You always do this shit! Break up, then come crying back to me, wanting to fix this shit. So, go ahead and pack yo' shit up then, Tyree." He laughed, lying back on the bed, flipping the TV on. "You'll be back. I'm not worried. All I gotta do is buy you some shit and you're good."

I stayed quiet, texting Noelle, asking if I could stay with her for the weekend. I continued to pack another bag before grabbing my coat and walking out of the room, laptop in hand. Ontrell closed the door to the room behind me.

"See you in a few days, nigga," he said, laughing as I walked out of the apartment.

As soon as I pulled up to Noelle's house, I sighed, seeing Shiloh's car parked behind her car. *Great*. Getting out of the car with my coat wrapped tightly around me, I saw her standing in the door way, holding it open so I could walk in.

"Did you eat?" she asked quietly as I set my things down in the living room. I knew her classy ass had taste in clothes, but her house décor was just as nice. She even had an air mattress ready and waiting for me on the living room floor, with blankets and a pillow.

"Yeah, I ate," I told her, looking around and seeing Shiloh's shoes in the corner. I smirked as I looked at her, standing there in her shorts and T-shirt, with her hair wrapped.

"What?" She laughed.

"So y'all fucking yet?" I pressed.

"Oh God, you sound like Layla." She sighed. "No, we haven't. Sometimes he likes to come over here and just sleep in my bed with me. Can't two people do that?"

"Uh, bitch, yo' dark chocolate ass needs to be making some cocoa babies with that vanilla nigga in there," I stated, and she laughed, hand on her chest. Just as I said it, I heard her door open, and Shiloh's fine ass stepped out of the room, shirtless, with his black basketball shorts hanging low. His muscular back flexes as he stretched, rubbing his eyes. He looked at me, eyes squinting, before tipping his head up in greeting.

"Heeey, Shiloh," I greeted as he walked to the kitchen. Noelle and I both just watched her man in awe. She knew he was fine. He was the finest Carter, in my opinion, after Ontrell. Jahiem and Talin could get it too, though.

He grabbed a glass of juice before walking back in the room, closing the door behind him. I slapped Noelle hard on the arm, and she winced in pain.

"Bitch, if you don't ride that nigga into the next year, some other full-time ho like Layla is going to do it for you," I snapped.

"Why would you use Layla as—"

"Because that ho wants him. He sees it; I see it. Everybody sees that shit but you. Better get it together, girl," I told her, plopping down on my air bed. "Now go, so I can cry in peace over my man."

"Oh Lord." She sighed with a smile. "If you need anything, just knock."

"I got you."

A Night To Remember

Taylor

"So, what happened?" I asked Olivia as we sat in her room on Saturday morning, eating a bowl of cereal. We were supposed to have her birthday party at the house that night, but finding out that her older brother Jahiem was in jail had put a damper on a few things. I sat on the edge of her bed in my red sorority pajama bottoms and a simple white tank, with my hair in a jumbo-sized twist. Her room was decorated with pictures of friends, family, and her sorority sisters. One wall had a pink-and-green frame around it. I wasn't that over the top with my colors, but when you walked in my room, you could tell I was the opposite of her sorority.

"I have no idea. Now Navier wants to come by and spend the night," she said excitedly, eyes wide as she looked at me. "What the fuck am I supposed to do?"

"I mean, he's yo' boyfriend, so at some point, he has to meet your brothers," I told her as she groaned, falling back on her bed. Navier was Olivia's boyfriend of damn near a year, and he had yet to meet her brothers. I had met him a while back when I came to visit from California. I didn't care for the nigga because he was a know-it-all and cocky as fuck, but if he made her happy, then that was all that mattered.

"I know they won't like him, just like I know he won't like them, and you know how he is. He doesn't hold back," she said, looking at her phone. "But I told myself I wanted to have sex for the first time on my birthday, and this is the perfect night to do it. I just need my brothers to stay away for a night," she said, mind turning with ideas before she looked at me with those sneaky hazel eyes. I already knew what the fuck she was thinking.

"No, no, and no," I told her, and she started pleading.

"Taylor! Come on! I would do it for you!"

"Bitch, I don't have a million brothers, and I wish I was having sex tonight!" I laughed, thinking about how I needed to get out. I refused to be the only virgin in this house after tonight. It was sad that Olivia and I were both not sexually active, but I had my reasons. She was always the gorgeous girl every nigga would kill over, so her having a boyfriend for a year with no sex was normal. They did shit like that for her, but for me? Nah.

"Just keep them occupied for the night," she begged, grabbing my arm as she gave me the puppy-dog face. I stared at my best friend of over twenty years, since diaper days. Looking at her dark complexion and those sleepy eyes, I thought she looked just like Elijah would if he was a girl.

"Who all is coming over here?" I sighed, and she squealed in excitement, hugging me.

"I think it's just Elijah and Trent," she said, looking at her phone. Lighting up as she smiled, she swiped the screen to answer it. "Hello?"

"What up?" Shiloh said through the speaker in a sleepy voice. "What you doing?"

"Laying in the bed with Tay, trying to figure out what we doing for the birthday. Did you call the boys?"

"Nah, not yet," he said softly into the phone just as we heard a female's voice in the background.

"Can you tell your hoes to keep quiet? It's not even eight in the morning, Shiloh," Olivia teased, and I laughed.

"Nah, I'm at my girlfriend's house right now. She's on the phone with her pops," he said easily, and both of our jaws dropped. This was the one nigga who did not believe in having a girlfriend. Like, that shit was unheard of.

"Girlfriend!" We both shrieked, hearing him laugh.

"Since when? Why haven't I met her? How long has this been going on, Shiloh?"

"It's new shit," he said in his usual calm manner. "Aye, look, I was calling to tell you happy birthday. I'll stop by later on to give you yo' birthday present."

"Nah-uh, back to the girl," Olivia said, and he laughed. "Do you like her? Like, really like her, or is this some temporary thing boys go through with girls? Is this just for cuffing season?"

"What the fuck is cuffing season, Olivia?" he asked, and I laughed. I forgot Shiloh was damn near close to thirty and didn't keep up with the trends. "Aye, look, I'm about to go. Have a happy twenty-fourth birthday, baby girl. I love you. don't turn up too hard tonight."

"Love you too, Shy," she said as they hung up. "I can't believe he has a girlfriend now. I can only imagine what type of girls he keeps around."

"Girl, who you telling?" I laughed as we got up. "We need to do some shopping. You need to find some sexy lingerie for your man, and I need to figure out what I'm supposed to do with your brothers for a whole night."

Later on that day, each of her brothers dropped a certain amount of money in her account, so she'd been getting text messages like crazy from her bank, due to the deposits. Of course, we spent the fuck out of that money, buying things for the house, food, and shoes that we could share. It was one of the perks of being best friends with a girl with seven brothers. We met up with her boyfriend at the mall, so with me being a typical third wheel, I made my way to another store, just keeping to myself, to let them do their thing. Like I said, I didn't fuck with her boyfriend like that. I ended up collecting a few numbers here and there, but the real shit was what was happening later on that night. Elijah and Trent were on their way over, and so was her boyfriend, Navier.

We had come up with a bulletproof plan that I just knew was going to work. We had already set the bait earlier by dropping hints to the boys that she wasn't feeling well, so by the time she got home, she got undressed, wore an oversized T-shirt and shorts, hair wrapped, and lay in the bed. Of course, underneath was a sexy red lingerie ensemble, ready for her boyfriend to unwrap. In the meantime, Elijah decided he wanted to go out to eat for his birthday with his girl. Trent's girlfriend wasn't in town, so guess who his date was? Me! I hadn't spoken to him since I first moved in, and we barely spoke then. It was just too awkward; too much tension between us, and I hated that. I never wanted it to be that way, but here I was, standing in the mirror, looking at my dress for the night. Double date with the twins.

"Are you nervous about being with Trent for the night?" Olivia asked as she popped into my room, sitting on the bed, eyeing my outfit.

"Girl, I told you we are grown. We should be past that high-school phase by now," I told her, turning to the side.

"But I know you, Taylor. You've been in love with Trent since way back when," she said knowingly as I looked at her, smiling.

"I didn't know what the fuck love was back then. I still don't." I laughed. "It was a crush, a serious crush."

"So, why you wearing this dress then?" she pointed out as we both looked at my reflection in the mirror. I had on a red, long-sleeve maxi dress that had a split coming up to my thigh, body-hugging every inch of my curves, and my hair was pulled up in a high bun. I had a black-and-gold clutch bag, with gold accessories and matching heels, light makeup, light lip color, smelling like sweet pea from Bath & Body Works.

"Is it too much?"

"Uh, it's perfect if you're trying to impress somebody!" She laughed.

"Whatever," I mumbled, looking at my nails to make sure they were on point.

Suddenly, there was a loud knock on the door that turned into a catchy beat. Elijah. Olivia quickly jumped up and rushed to her room, already trying to cough as she closed the door.

"Don't let them in here!" she hissed from behind the door as I walked to the living room.

As soon as I pulled the door open, I saw Elijah and Trent standing there with smiles. Their eyes started to roam.

"Aye, you better be glad I look at you like another sister, man," Elijah let out, licking his lips.

"What is that supposed to mean?" I laughed as I reached out to hug him.

"It means if I didn't look at you like fam, and I didn't have my girl coming with us tonight, you would have been fucked by me," he stated as I pushed his nasty ass away from me, laughing. He was never one to hold his tongue.

"You guys look nice," I noted, eyeing Trent, who dressed up in slacks, collared shirt, bow tie, and a matching blazer. He had a clean, hairless face, with a fresh cut and those sexy eyes, those sexy hazel eyes. Damn! Elijah, on the other hand, didn't bother. He kept it true to himself, wearing all black: black long-sleeve V-neck showing that tatted chest, black leather-like harem pants, with black Gucci sneakers and a black jacket. His locs were pulled up in a wild, sloppy ball, and he had shades on like he was the hottest nigga in the middle of the night.

"Where Livie at?" Elijah asked, already walking to the back room. "Olivia! Yo' ass ain't fucking sick on yo' birthday! I know you up to something else with yo' faking ass!"

I smirked before turning my attention back to Trent, who couldn't stop staring.

"So, where's your girlfriend, birthday boy?" I asked, trying to break the ice.

"She's in New York for the weekend. We already celebrated my shit a few days ago."

"Oh, yeah? That's cool," I said, nodding slowly as my eyes started from his shoes and moved up slowly. "You look really nice, Trenton Michael Carter."

"Come on, man." He laughed slowly. "You ain't gotta call my name out like that."

"Just sayin'." I shrugged with a laugh as Elijah came walking back.

"Y'all finish eye-fucking each other or nah?" Elijah asked, stepping in between us to walk out the door.

"Oh Lord, this is going to be a long-ass night," I mumbled, grabbing my coat and bag.

"Ooooo weee! It's colder than a bitch from New York out here!" Elijah let out as Trent cut his eyes at him before getting in the passenger's seat. Of course, they would have me sitting in the back because they didn't have no fucking sense. I just prayed whoever the girl was that Elijah was bringing could hold a conversation. And I hoped Olivia got the best sex of her life that night, because she owed me big time for this one. I could only handle but so much of Elijah's hyper ass before I started to get irritated.

"Aye, you remember the time we all went to Auntie Faye's house and stole all her shit out the fridge?" Elijah asked, and I laughed at the memory. "Maaan, Trent's slow ass was trying to be picky about what to get."

"If I'm going to get caught stealing some bullshit, it better be worth my fucking time, nigga," Trent retorted.

"Or the time Elijah got suspended for trying to pull Ms. Howard's pants down in front of everybody?" I added as we all laughed.

"I forgot about her fine ass," Elijah said thoughtfully as he turned down a street. "Yo, she was hitting on me. I don't give a fuck what anyone says. Bitch wanted the D."

"I can't believe we're grownups now," I said, crossing my legs as I stared out the window, looking out into the night. "Twenty-four years old."

"Hell yeah, can't believe I made it to see twenty-four," Elijah said quietly, deep in thought as we pulled into a neighborhood behind a university.

"You made it, bruh," Trent said, bringing Elijah's head in close before letting go.

I smiled at the small but cute exchange. Despite them being polar opposites, all three triplets were closer than any family I'd ever seen before.

"I missed you guys." I smiled as Elijah glanced back at me with a smile. "Despite how y'all used to get on me, I did miss y'all."

"I think Trent might have missed you a little bit more," Elijah said, and Trent punched him in the arm. "Nigga, fuck did I say?"

"Why you always gotta start shit?"

"Aye, tell her what you told me before pulling up to her house, nigga."

My eyes lit up, watching the two start to argue while pulling up to a small house with the porch light on.

"What did you say, Trent?"

"I didn't say—"

"He said!" Elijah interjected, and I laughed. "He wished he would have never treated you like that back in high school, but don't know how to fucking apologize to you now because he's scared to talk to you."

"Bruh, I didn't say it like that!"

"That's how I took it." He shrugged before hopping out. "Get yo' ass in the back seat with her so my bitch can sit with me, nigga."

"You didn't say that?" I questioned as Trent got out with a groan. He was never one to admit when he was wrong. He would go through hell and back before admitting he was in the wrong, or even apologizing.

When he sat in the back with me, I felt my body respond immediately to the closeness.

"I said it, but not like that. I do want to apologize, because I don't want shit to be awkward between us," he said, looking me in my eyes as I smiled.

"Look, it's the past," I said, waving him off. "We were young and dumb. We're grown adults, and hopefully you don't see me as that little big girl, because I don't see you as that bad-ass hazel-eyed boy anymore."

"Nah." He laughed smoothly, licking his lips. Shit, my body got the chills from that.

"Just a simple man and woman that can work toward being friends," I stated, and he nodded.

"I'm good with that," he agreed, and we shook hands.

"So, what's your girlfriend like?" I asked out of curiosity.

With a shake of his head, he said, "She's different." He shrugged easily, with a small smile. "Mean as fuck, but can be a sweetheart when she wants to be."

"Aww," I cooed. "What's her major? Does she want to be a lawyer like you?"

"Nah, I don't know what she's trying to do. I don't think she knows either, to be honest. She not really thinking about that," he said, and I smirked.

Well, that's attractive.

"What about you?" he asked, turning his body toward mine.

I just looked at my nails, lips pursed, with a smile. "I have no one. Single as can be," I said, shrugging.

"Are you looking? A couple of my frat brothers will definitely get at you," he said, and I laughed.

"Nigga, I vowed never to date another frat boy. I want someone outside of the Greek life. I'm caught up in it; I don't want the nigga I'm with to be caught up in it as well. Besides, I'm going to start getting out in the city on my own soon, date a little bit, have a little fun."

"You telling me Big Tay about to go on a fucking spree?" he asked, and we both laughed, with me playfully hitting him.

"I wish." I sighed. "I still have my innocence about me. About ready to throw that shit away. Can't be twenty-four and still a virgin. You know how many friends, all my sorors, everyone around me is having sex, talking about sex, and I'm the one left out of the loop because I haven't done it yet?"

He stared at me in silent shock just as Elijah's phone went off. Only then did we realize we were still sitting in the truck.

"Where the fuck is yo' brother at?"

We looked at the door to the house, seeing him walking with a girl behind him as she closed the door. Elijah looked upset, and she looked . . . I couldn't even read her face, but Elijah was definitely not in the mood.

When they got in, I immediately went to looking her over, trying to judge the girl before she opened her mouth. She definitely wasn't all the way black, not with that wet, curly hair. She wore jeans with heels and a cute top, with her hair slicked back in a high ponytail, cascading down her back. She was matching Elijah's casual style for the night. Right off the bat, I knew it was her real hair. She had a brown-like complexion and was slim, but thick with it. Shit, that's where I was trying to be.

"So, when did he come by?" Elijah asked, backing out of the driveway as she looked at him, resting her chin on her hand.

"Does it matter? I handled it."

"But why the fuck does he know where you live, Jordyn?" he snapped, causing me to jump.

"Aye, not on the birthday, bruh. Come on now," Trent chimed in.

The car fell into a tense, awkward silence as Trent pulled out his phone, tapping my thigh to get my number. As soon as the exchange was made, we sat in silence, texting each other, making fun of Elijah and this Jordyn chick. All you could hear was us trying so hard not to crack up, with small snickers escaping our lips.

I texted him: SO WAT DO U WANT 4 UR BDAY?

I waited for his response as he looked out the window in thought before texting me back.

He answered: I REALLY WNT SUM BDAY SEX BUT CNT GET IT UNTIL SHE GETS BAK.

I TEXTED BACK: NIGGA U NASTY. ONLY U WUD THINK ABOUT SEX ON UR BDAY WHEN U CAN GET IT N E DAY. LOL LEAST U GETTING SUM.

Trent let out a laugh before his thumbs went to typing on his screen: U CUD GET SUM IF U TRIED TAY. U GOT A BANGIN BODY, UR GORGEOUS, AND U COOL AS FUK. U ACTIN LIKE NO NIGGA WUD WANNA HIT IT. I WUD...

I stared at that last part of the message hard. Shit, if I wasn't throbbing down below in my panties, my heart was throbbing in my chest. I told myself, *Keep it calm, Taylor. This nigga will only be a friend, and nothing more.*

I texted: ITS JUST I DNT FEEL COMFORTABLE BEING COMPLETELY NAKED IN FRONT OF A NIGGA. IF I CUD KEEP MY PANTIES N SHIRT ON DURIN SEX, I WILL B GUD. LOL

He answered: NAH, ALL OF DAT WILL COME OFF IF IT WAS ME. LOL REAL TLK

Then I said: NIGGA U TALKIN LIKE U WANT IT. LMAO

He shot back: I DO.

I damn near dropped my phone as I looked up at him. Trent just shrugged, licking his lips— those fucking lips—and smirked.

"Aye, when y'all finish sexting each other, we inside eating," Elijah said from outside the car before closing the door. I looked around, seeing we were already at the Cheesecake Factory at Cumberland Mall.

"Stay put. I got the door," Trent said quickly as he got out, rushing to the other side to open my door.

I stepped out, taking his waiting hand before he closed the door. "Nigga, you trying to put game on ol' Big Tay," I teased, and he laughed.

"Nah, it's just been a minute since I went out to eat with a woman like this. Trying to play my part. My girlfriend don't really do shit like this."

"I bet," I mumbled as we stepped inside the packed restaurant, looking around for Elijah and Jordyn. Trent kept his hand on my lower back, guiding me to the small booth where Elijah sat with his girlfriend, arm around her neck, kissing her affectionately as she smiled. Sliding in the seat across from them, I actually got a look at her face for the first time. She was naturally pretty, but could use some makeup here and there. Her eyes were stunning, though.

"What color are your eyes?" I asked, leaning in.

"Gray. Last time I checked they were light gray, but they may have gotten darker," she said with a small shrug.

"What are you mixed with?" I asked curiously, looking her over completely.

"My father is Mexican, and my mother is black and white," she said, and my mouth dropped. She was basically the essence of America.

"Yeah, I can definitely see the Mexican in you," I said, nodding my head. That explained all that damn hair.

We ordered our food and had small talk about school, family, and just life goals. I shared some childhood stories with Jordyn about what it was like growing up with these two fools. It was actually not a bad time. Elijah, and Jordyn definitely complimented each other. She calmed him down tremendously, and I would occasionally catch him looking at her, just staring at her while she spoke to me. I didn't know what the deal was between her and Trent, but it was obvious she didn't care for him.

Then, as always, it turned into sex. Conversation always seemed to turn to sex.

"Yo, you remember our eleventh birthday?" Elijah asked Trent, who started to laugh. "Bruh, that was probably the craziest night I ever experienced."

"What happened?" Jordyn asked, taking a bite of her pasta as I sat back, ready to hear the story. The restaurant was noisy, but it felt like we were still in our own bubble.

"You telling the story or am I?" Trent asked, putting his arm around my neck.

"I'll tell it, because you be fucking exaggerating like hell. So, look," Elijah started, clearing his throat, trying to be so dramatic. "It was our birthday, and Shiloh was like, what y'all trying to do for your birthday? I'm like, I want some fucking money, bruh." He put his hand out as he acted out the story. "I'll be straight. Get me a bag of weed and some money, and I'm good."

"You were smoking at that age, Elijah?" Jordyn asked, and I laughed.

"Fuck yeah. So, he was like 'Nah, it's time y'all know the true meaning of being a man. Need to learn what makes the world go around and what makes niggas do what the fuck we do. You rolling with the big homies tonight,' " Elijah continued, mocking Shiloh's deep voice.

"Who all was with you?" I asked.

"He got me, Trent, and Talin in the car, and we met up with Anthony and Jahiem. These mothafuckas took us to a hotel room, ordered drinks, dancers, and those dancers brought their homegirls over. We weren't supposed to tell them our age. For all they knew, I think we said we was turning sixteen?" Elijah questioned, looking at Trent for confirmation. Trent nodded in agreement. "So, we getting lap dances, throwing money to the bitches, drinking, and Anthony let it be known that we were all virgins. So, the chicks started laughing, while one of them came to me and asked me straight-up do I want to know what it feels like to be insider of her. I was like, bruh? I damn near nutted on myself at the fucking question!" he said, and we laughed. "All I could do was nod my head like, yeah, trying to be cool. So, she took my hand and led me out to the next room. Next thing I know, Talin and Trent came in with their girls, and all three of us got fucked by them that night. I mean, I came like seconds after being inside, but that night damn near changed my life," he said as Trent laughed.

"All we talked about on the ride back home was sex," Trent said as I laughed. "Compared the girls to each other; we talked about who lasted longer, knowing damn well none of us went beyond ten seconds. Shiloh told us not to say a word to Mama, but Pops already knew the moment he saw us that same weekend. He knew what was up. What did he say to us, E?"

"Nigga said,"—he cleared his throat with a fist to his chest before looking sternly at us— "you are now officially Carter men," he mocked, with Trent laughing.

"Stupid, bruh. That was a crazy-ass night."

"Hell yeah!" Elijah laughed as he slapped hands with his brother. "Best birthday I ever had, nigga."

"So, that's some type of tradition or . . . ?" I cut in curiously.

"Shit, we'on know. Pops said he and his brothers did it."

"That's so sick," Jordyn said in disgust. "How old were the girls?"

"Probably eighteen or nineteen. Maybe in their twenties."

"I hope my first time isn't as bad as that," I mumbled, and they all looked at me. Trent gave me a sneaky smile, Jordyn sat there with her mouth dropped, and Elijah cut his eyes between Trent and me.

"And on that note, it's time to go," I said, getting up as we all laughed.

Piling into his truck once again, Elijah lit up one of the longest joints I'd ever seen in my life and passed it around, letting everyone take a hit. Jordyn passed on the second round, still coughing from the first hit, while Trent and I enjoyed it together.

"Nigga, you cheesing hard as hell right now," I said, giggling.

"You gon' let me take it?" he asked on the hush-hush, careful not to tip Elijah's nosey ass off.

"I'm like a sister to you," I retorted as he shook his head.

"Aww, come on," he groaned playfully, head falling back on the seat as Elijah pulled up to a gas station. It was perfect timing, too. I needed a drink or two.

"Hey, how about Jordyn and I go in on a bottle for y'all birthday?" I suggested, hoping I hadn't put Jordyn on the spot.

"Shit, cool with me," Elijah cheesed at Jordyn. "You know what we always get, baby."

"E&J," she said coolly, opening the door.

I smiled, thinking about their initials for their name.

"Nobody wants that hood-ass drink but you two," Trent let out, and I laughed, getting out of the car.

I walked inside with Jordyn, smoothing my hair up as we caught the attention of every living soul in the damn gas station, smack down in the middle of the hood, middle of the night. The only people that hung around gas stations were drunks, bums, and niggas trying to move product.

"So, you and Elijah . . ." I started as I followed her to the back. "I guess y'all have an open relationship?"

"We do."

"Nobody is getting their feelings caught up?" I pressed as we stood in front of the assortment of drinks.

"It's hard to say. I think he is starting to but won't admit it," she said casually, grabbing the bottle.

I grabbed a thing of Grey Goose, and as we attempted to pay for it, the man was so . . . appreciative of our looks that he let us get away with both bottles for free if we promised to come back. Walking out, I could see Elijah standing at the gas pump, filling his tank up, shades on his head as he leaned against his truck, eyes only for Jordyn.

"I'll take your bag," I told her, seeing she was already heading toward him and didn't plan on getting in the car. They were in love with each other. It was obvious to anyone who could see. Nigga looked at her like she was his everything.

"You ready for bed, baby?" he asked her as he pulled her close, already wrapping his arms around her tight. I got in the back with Trent, already popping the bottle.

"I bet," I started, taking a small swig from the bottle. "I bet you wouldn't even know what to do with all this thickness, nigga."

"Oh yeah?" He smirked, taking the bottle from me. "Unless you trying to find out, we don't have nothing to talk about, Tay. You scared."

"I'm not scared!" I laughed as the front doors opened, with both Elijah and Jordyn hopping in their seats.

"Where my drink at?"

"Nah-uh, nigga, you can't drink and drive," I told him, handing the E&J to Jordyn. "You already know you gotta be the sober one."

"I can hold my alcohol,"

"Nope. Jordyn, don't let him drink just yet," I demanded as he snatched the bottle from Jordyn's hands.

"Fuck that! It's my birthday. I can do whatever the fuck I want to do. I'm getting drunk and high at the same time while driving, and best believe I'm getting this dick wet tonight, so fuck everything else," Elijah stated as he and Trent slapped hands.

"Ayyee! That's what the fuck I'm talking about! Me too!" Trent let out, and I cocked my head at him.

"Who wetting yo' dick, nigga? Yo' girl is in New York."

"You are," he stated, blowing a kiss at me as I laughed nervously. "I'm gonna get it tonight. You know I am. I don't even know why you playing like you don't want me."

"Because I don't," I said, crossing my legs.

"Yeah, okay," he snorted.

The moment we reached Olivia's house, I spotted only her car and my car in the driveway, so I just assumed her boyfriend was gone for the night. I couldn't wait to hear the details of her night.

"Aye," Elijah said as he rolled the window down on his car door. "Trent, hit me up when you get back home, nigga," he said, smirking as he cut his eyes to me.

"Oh my God, Elijah, nothing is going to happen between us, especially at y'all sister's house." I laughed, walking to the door. Looking back, I could see Elijah telling Trent something as they both cracked identical smiles at the same time before laughing. *Niggas.*

I opened the door to the dark house, hearing music coming from Olivia's room. Bitch must have had a good-ass night. Setting my coat down, I slipped off my heels and headed straight for my room, with Trent no doubt coming in behind me shortly after.

"Aye," he whispered softly as he came into my room, closing the door behind him. "You mind if I spend the night? I really do just want to sleep. I won't try you or nothing. If you not trying to have sex, then I can't pressure you."

I just stared at this fine piece of art—tall, light caramel skin, with those eyes and lips. I didn't even want to know what he looked like naked.

"Do you still snore?" I asked, and he smiled sheepishly. *Ugh*.

"Nigga, get on in the bed and keep quiet. I don't want Olivia knowing you still here. She's going to think we doing something," I said.

"Where you about to go?" he asked, undoing his shirt.

I grabbed a towel out of my closet, a long T-shirt with the California state flag on it, and some panties.

"I'm about to take a quick shower," I said, walking out. "Don't go through my shit."

Let me tell y'all, that might have been the quickest shower I ever took. I don't know what caused me to even shave down there like I was getting some that night, but damn it if I didn't take extra care of my goods in that shower. Looking at myself in the mirror, I stayed bra-less, 'fro wild and all over the place; feet were freshly done in a simple red-and-white French manicure to match my fingernails. I wiped my face free of makeup and dabbed very light perfume on in certain corners of my body. *Nigga, if you're going to sleep in my bed, best believe you're going to wake up smelling like me.*

Smiling to myself in the mirror, I pushed my breasts up for a quick pump and walked out, switching the light off. Olivia had that sex playlist on repeat. I almost wanted to go in her room to cut it off for her, but I was going to mind my own business. Let her rest for now.

Walking to my room, I opened the door, seeing this fool laying in my bed, wearing only Superman boxer briefs. His body was cut to a T! That dick was sitting to the side on his thigh like it was on sleep mode. Damn, I wasn't prepared for this. He looked up at me, smiling, hand behind his head as he scrolled through his phone.

"You look like you scared to lay next to me, Big Tay," he said with a laugh, eyes resting on my thighs before slowly looking me over. "You got pretty feet."

"Thank you. And where the fuck are yo' clothes at?" I pressed, voice breaking as I closed the door behind me, cutting the light off.

"It's too hot to sleep with that shit on. Same reason why you don't have none on."

"All I know is you better take yo' ass straight to bed, Trenton," I warned as I lay down on my side of the bed, closest to the window.

We lay there in awkward silence as he put his phone up on the nightstand. Feeling him move about underneath my covers, leg hitting mine, I silently cursed myself, biting my lower lip to keep from speaking out.

"Can I ask you a question, though?" he asked as I turned to look at him, wondering how his voice had become even deeper. Maybe it was my mind fucking with me. Had to be.

"What?"

"Why do you want to have sex with your clothes on? Isn't the whole experience about physically connecting with that person, body for body, touch for touch, lick for lick, all that?" he asked as I closed my eyes.

"I just . . . my body isn't where I would want it to be, so until I get—"

"Yo' body is fine, Taylor. You never used to be insecure about—"

"I've always been insecure about my body, and you out of anyone should know why," I snapped, and he became silent. "So, if I can't have sex with a man who doesn't mind me keeping my shirt on and just sliding the panties to the side, I'm good."

"That's the kind of nigga you don't want to fuck with. You gotta get someone that's going to appreciate your body, every inch, every curve, everything. Some niggas like breasts, and some like thighs. Why cover that shit up? Why deny the man the one thing he loves about a woman?"

"You don't get it," I mumbled, turning over on my side. *Can we stop talking about fucking sex, though? Like, really? I'm laying next to the man I've been feeling from day one. He's naked with a body like the gods, I'm naked, and we're talking about sex?*

"I do get it," he answered back. "I can show you how much I get it if you let me."

"Trenton, stop!" I hissed, hearing him laugh. It had to be the alcohol. "You have a girlfriend."

"A'ight, I'm going to stop fucking with you." He laughed. "But my dick is hard as fuck right now, tho—" I got up from the bed, hearing his childish-ass laugh as I cut the lights on, standing near the door, arms folded. I know my hair must have looked crazy because I didn't bother to twist it down, but I wanted this nigga out. It was the only thing I was concerned about.

Yet when Trent looked at me, licking his lips, hazel eyes heavy in arousal, and . . . I don't know. Something just clicked in me. I don't know if it was how he was looking me over like I was the sexiest woman in the world, or the fact that he was hard and I could see that shit lined up along his thigh.

"Okay," I mumbled, looking down at the floor nervously before peeking at him. "Show me."

He immediately got up, hands cupping my face, and kissed me, pressing my back up against the door as my hands came to grip his waist.

The very first kiss between us, and everything about it, sent chills throughout my body as we connected. Suddenly, I felt him bend down like he was about to lift me.

"No, no, no, you can't pick me up," I freaked as he grabbed me tight, lifting me off the floor like I was a sack of feathers.

He cut the lights off and took me to bed like it was nothing. Laying in between my legs, he reached over to cut the lamp light on then reached down below, grabbing a condom out of his wallet. I couldn't believe I was about to have sex. I couldn't believe this shit.

"Why do we need the light?" I pressed, wanting it off.

"So I can see what I'm doing to you," was all he said as he placed the condom on the nightstand before placing himself in between me comfortably. "Take this hot-ass shirt off, Taylor."

"I'm keeping it on," I stated, arms folded across my chest.

"Nah, I can't fuck with clothes on, Tay."

"Well, I can."

"You not even big like that! I don't know why you so worried about how yo' body looks. It's not that serious. We grown. You grown."

He started lifting my shirt up. We immediately started fighting for pulling rights before he finally lifted it up completely over my head, revealing nothing but breasts and stomach. I quickly covered myself as he looked me over, no smile. His body was so fit, so toned, that when he placed himself over me again, I couldn't even make eye contact. I felt so . . . I didn't feel sexy at all. If this nigga would just cut the fucking lights off, all this could be solved.

"So, you really going to avoid looking at me while I'm doing this?" he asked in a casual voice.

"Nigga, just hurry up. You already pissed me off; got me laying here with no fucking shirt on," I mumbled, arms covering myself up some more.

"Spread yo' legs some more," he commanded, looking down between us. "Come on. Quit being a baby about this, Tay."

I opened up a little more, feeling him place himself completely on top of me.

"A'ight, so you can act like a brat all you want, but we doing this. No going back now. Quit doing that shit," he said, moving my arms away from my body. "I told you I don't have a problem with yo' body."

"Yes, you do," I mumbled, trying to cover myself.

"Taylor, you trying the fuck out of me right now. Stop doing that shit. I'm serious," he said in a stern voice.

I let my arms fall weakly to my side as I looked up at the ceiling, feeling tears about to come down. *Why now, and why him?*

"Can you look at me?" he asked, voice getting low as I shook my head no, looking up at the ceiling. It wasn't until I felt him pinch at my sides that I looked down at him, mouth dropped.

"Nigga, you—"

"You got a few extra pounds to you. So the fuck what?" he teased, pulling at my stomach.

"That don't mean pinch my shit, nigga. You making it worse!" I snapped, feeling the tears fall as he looked at me.

"Why are you so sensitive about it all of a sudden?" He laughed before realizing I was actually crying. He let out a sigh as he came up closer so our faces were eye to eye as he looked at me. "Aye, real shit though, Taylor?"

"What, nigga?" I mumbled, wiping my cheeks. "You gonna tell me how fat I used to be, or how I still am?"

"Nah." He smiled, hazel eyes piercing down into my dark brown eyes.

This nigga here, and those damn eyes.

"Then what, Trenton?"

"My dick is hard as fuck right now," he stressed as we both looked down between us, seeing his dick sticking straight out underneath the

Superman briefs. "You wanna cry and feel insecure about yo' body, but trust me, this dick don't
get hard for just any female."

"Shut up, Trent," I snapped as we both looked
at each other before bursting into a small fit of
laughter.

"Can we do this?" he questioned. "Are you
ready? I'm supposed to show you what it's like."

I nodded slowly.

"You don't know where yo' hot spots are?"

I could feel my body respond just off that
statement alone, but everything was telling me
to focus on what was between my legs.

"I don't think so," I said slowly, feeling him
place himself between me again, resting on me.
"Maybe my breasts?"

His eyes lit up with a smile as his eyes went to
the nipple on the right.

"Or the neck?" I said, watching his eyes shift to
my neck like he was thinking, plotting.

"We're just going to cover it all. If you not
feeling it, tell me. If you are, I'll know."

"How will you know?" I asked just as he dove
in, lifting my chin up, and immediately went
for my neck, biting down gently. I let out a gasp,
feeling chills go throughout my body.

My hands gripped his sides as he moved lower,
taking care of each breast like they were his.

I felt his hands tug at my panties, our breathing becoming labored. Oh, shit! It was about to get real.

"Can I take em off, Tay?" he asked, eyes heavy.

I nodded, getting ready to place my hand in between my legs.

"I swear, if you cover yourself with yo' hands, I'm walking the fuck out."

I nodded again.

He slid my panties off, looking down as he smiled. "I can't believe we really about to do this shit."

"Nigga, don't stare at it!" I snapped, and he laughed.

He took a finger, sliding down between me as his mouth dropped. "Shit, you been ready for me," he mumbled, taking his underwear off with super speed.

I tried, really I tried, not to look at his dick, but the cream-stick was calling my name, and as soon as I saw its thickness, standing long and prideful, I flipped.

"That's not going to work," I said quickly, backing up.

"I know what the fuck I'm doing," he stated, grabbing my ankle to pull me back. "Chill out, Tay." I watched him roll the condom on, and then he placed himself in between. "Hold on to me. If I'm hurting you, tell me to stop."

I nodded as I gripped his shoulders.

As we stared at each other, he smirked. "You ready?"

"No, I'm not—" I shut my eyes tight, feeling him press into me. That sharp pain had me digging my nails in this nigga's skin so quick. "Trent!"

"Relax. You gotta relax," he said with his mouth against my cheek. "You tense as hell right now."

"Nigga, you relax!" I snapped, feeling him spread my thighs out further as he buried his face in my neck and shoulder. Feeling him press into me again, I wrapped my arms tight around his neck, trying my hardest not to cry. "Trent, please," I begged. I let out a gasp, feeling him completely push himself inside of me, hearing him let out a curse against my ear.

"Just let it sit," he mumbled as my body adjusted to the foreign object. He lifted his head up to become eye level with me. "You ready?"

"Yeah," I said, nodding my head as I felt him move ever so slowly. "Don't go any faster than this," I told him.

His eyes were closed as he nodded, caught in the moment. It honestly felt like nothing for the first couple of seconds, but either he shifted or changed strokes, and suddenly I felt a dose of pleasure with each pull and push. He occasionally glanced at me for confirmation.

"You good?" He breathed as my head went back, nodding in response. "Cool. relax a little bit," he commanded, lifting my legs up high, spreading them wider as he started dunking himself in and out, watching his work.

"Deeper," I called out, barely above a whisper, but he came down on me, my knees pushed back toward the bed as he pushed himself further in me, causing me to cry out. That was it. Right there, that was the fucking spot. I could feel that shit.

"Can you teach me how to ride?" I asked in between breaths as he looked at me, pulling out slowly. I had watched enough videos to know the basics, but I wanted to learn based on experience.

"Come here," he said in a deep voice as he lay back, guiding me to sit directly on it, sliding down as he gripped my hips, moving my body for me. I followed his lead before getting the hang of it, taking a pace of my own. My hands pressed down on his pecs as he slapped, gripped, and pulled at my ass in his own excitement.

"Shit!" he hissed, biting his lower lip as he watched me. "You look sexy as fuck right now and don't even realize it."

"Shut up, Trent," I breathed, trying not to laugh as I slowed down.

We caught each other's eyes for a brief moment before he wrapped an arm around my waist and flipped me back over with ease. I let him take complete control before finally succumbing to the climactic end.

"Shit," he mumbled in a shaky voice as he hovered over me. "Aye, we just fucking had sex."

I looked at him as we stared at each other before bursting out into another small fit of laughter, with his face coming to mine. His lips were so close to mine we could have kissed if we wanted to.

"This can never happen again. You know that, right?" I told him, watching him take care of the condom.

"Shit, I'm the one with a girlfriend. I know it can't happen again," he agreed as we continued to laugh. "I had sex with Big Tay."

"Nigga, you need to stop calling me that," I snapped, hearing him laugh against my face.

"So, now the next nigga you get with has to top me," he declared as I let out a snort.

"I'm sure you won't be the best I ever had, Trent. Don't flatter yourself. You're good, but you won't be the best," I told him, feeling him pinch at my side. "Nigga, quit playing! I'm serious!" I laughed, playfully pushing him off me as he collapsed down beside me. "My body is going to be so sore tomorrow. Definitely gotta go to the gym in the morning."

"Hell yeah," he agreed as we fell silent, reliving every moment that had just happened between us.

Turning over, I pulled the covers over me, letting reality set in. *I really just had sex with my best friend's brother—some random chick in New York's boyfriend. Damn.*

I could hear him getting up, sliding on his boxer briefs as he stepped out to use the bathroom and officially clean himself up. Fuck it, I was too tired. My legs felt like they were stuck on wide gap mode right now. I could barely close my thighs.

When he came back to the bed, closing the door, without any other words to say to each other, we fell asleep, leaving space in the middle for the distance we needed to place between us.

So, perfect way to end a perfect night, right? Wrong as hell. It had to be three-something in the morning. I don't know what the fuck time it was, but I felt Trent nearly jump out of the bed as he sat up, stiff as a board, dark figure of his body with the light from the window bouncing off off it, still and quiet.

"Nigga, what the fuck—"

"Shhh," he hissed, and I became quiet.

Suddenly, I heard the sound of Olivia talking, almost like she was going off on someone.

"I said no, Navier!" she shouted, and my heart started to pound. *No, no, no, bitch! Is this nigga still at the damn house?*

I sat up, hearing what sounded like a thump, like something hit the wall hard.

"Because I fucking said so, nigga! If I don't want to do that, then I don't want to do it!"

"You acting like a spoiled bitch right now. I waited a fucking year to get some, and you won't even let me do what the fuck I want? After waiting this long? Fuck that," Navier stated as Trent got up, cutting the light on.

"Trent, don't—"

"Let go of me, Navier! I'm not fucking playing with you!" Olivia cried out.

Shit! I got up, trying to put on some clothes as Trent swung my door open and went straight to his sister's room, trying to open the door.

"Olivia!" he shouted as I walked out behind him, shorts and shirt on. "Open the fucking door!"

"So, you called yo' bitch-ass brothers over here?" Navier let out as everything about Trent's preppy, boyish personality went straight hood in that moment. Standing there in his Superman boxer briefs, nigga was on one right now.

Shit, let me get my sneakers, because if that nigga laid a hand on my girl, I was putting hands to that nigga's soul. We will be having funeral services for his whack ass on Sunday.

The door opened, with Olivia coming out, wearing her lingerie, tears in her eyes as she tried to keep Trent from going in the room.

"What the fuck are you doing here, Trent?"

"Who is that in there, and why doesn't he understand the meaning of no?" Trent asked, pushing his way into the room, walking straight up to Navier, who was Trent's equal in terms of height and body size. They were the exact same. "Bruh, we got a problem, nigga?"

"Ain't no problem, bruh!" Navier stepped up as they squared off. "This is between her and me. Get the fuck—"

"She is me, my nigga! Her problem is my problem!" Trent snapped, pushing dude back hard as Olivia screamed, trying to grab her brother. Navier regained his balanced after being pushed into her dresser and swung at Trent.

"Taylor, get Trent! Grab him!" she cried out as I tried pulling Trent and Navier apart, with Olivia coming to her boyfriend's aid. Navier, probably out of rage for Trent, was careless enough to push Olivia back off him, and she hit the wall hard.

"You defending this nigga over yo' own flesh and blood?" Trent shrieked. "You let him put his hands on you?"

"Trent, you gotta stop!" I pressed, trying to hold him back as Olivia slid to the carpet, crying hard, head buried in her knees. "Let them—"

"You see what the fuck you started, Olivia?" Navier screamed at her, going in as Trent pushed me aside, coming for him once more as they wrestled on the bed, blow for blow. Neither one of them would back down.

I quickly grabbed a hold of Trent, seeing Navier's eye was fucked up, but Trent's lip was bleeding just as bad. With Olivia getting off her crying ass to grab her boyfriend, I was able to pull Trent away and drag his crazy ass out the room.

"Go sit down in the living room!" I demanded, pushing him toward the couch. He sat down, heated. I knew him well enough to know he needed space and quiet to calm himself down. Grabbing his things out of my room, I went to check on Olivia, who was trying to apologize to Navier. When she saw me, she immediately went the fuck off like I was the one who had started all of this.

"Why is my brother still here?" she yelled, walking toward me. Her hair was a wreck, face was drained, and eyes were red with old and new tears. "Did you sleep with him?"

"Why you letting this nigga hit you, and why the fuck is he still here? After how he made it seem like he was about to fucking rape you, Olivia—"

"Aye, get the fuck out!" Navier snapped at me, and I cocked my head back.

"Bruh, you don't want it with me, nigga." I laughed sarcastically. "I'll beat yo' fucking ass like you stole something, nigga. Trust! Don't let this pretty face fool you!"

"Taylor, don't talk to him—"

"Are you serious, Olivia? Over this whack nigga?" I snapped, dropping Trent's clothes just as he came up behind me.

"Fuck her, Taylor! She act like she know every fucking thing. You can't see when you dealing with a fuck-ass nigga?" Trent snapped as Navier stood up, ready to do battle.

"Get out! Both of you! I'm grown! You can't keep treating me like a child!" Olivia cried out.

"You grown, but you stupid as fuck," Trent retorted, walking off. "I'm done! You think you know everything with yo' dumb ass. You on yo' own! Let that nigga beat on you!"

Olivia slammed the door hard in my face as I stood there, shaking my head. I knew she always had an issue with her brothers babying her, but this shit was to the extreme. She couldn't tell when she had a lame nigga by her side, because she was too busy trying to prove to everyone else that she was grown.

No, bitch, you ain't Beyoncé.

"Let's go. Take me the fuck home, bruh. I'm not fucking with her childish ass," Trent snapped as I quickly grabbed my coat and keys.

As soon as I dropped him off without so much as a goodbye to me, the girl he just had sex with, I headed back home. I was thinking this shit would soon blow over, but nah. Fuck nah. It was never like that dealing with these Carters.

When I got home, I could hear Olivia crying, and I saw glass all on the carpet leading to her room. Creeping through the hallway, careful not to step on the broken bits of glass, I pushed her door open and saw her face was fucked up. Her hands were bruised and bleeding, and her lip was busted. She had put up a fight, and I was pissed I let my emotions get the best of me, because I should have been right there, fighting alongside my bestie.

Looking around the room, I saw no trace of the bitch nigga. Navier was nowhere in sight. Looking at me, swollen cheek almost pushing her left eye closed, she shook her head.

"Please don't tell my brothers," she mumbled, tears coming down.

A Fan Favorite

Elijah

The Wild Nigga

"Aye, this yo' boy Jodie Carter with the Carter Boys, and you are tuned in to the people's station, V103," the radio let out, and I turned over in my bed in annoyance. I hated hearing myself on the fucking radio. But with that going off, it only reminded me that it was time to get up and do what the fuck I needed to do before I left for New York that night.

I'm not going to introduce myself, because y'all so far into the story that you should know who the fuck I be. You feel me? Elijah Jodie mothafucking Carter. Only Carter that matters in this book.

Barely opening my eyes, I looked at my girl lying next to me, hair all over the place from the crazy sex she stayed throwing at me every time

I was with her for a night. Last night was no different. Celebrating my twenty-fourth birthday, we purposely didn't set no plans for Saturday night in terms of music. I'd traveled from club to club all week, so Saturday, I wanted to be left in peace and in the arms of my girl by the end of the night. All that partying shit gets played out after a while.

Moving her hair out of her face, I smirked, seeing her open one eye. Mouth opened, drool on the side, she was naked as she tucked her arms underneath the pillows, rubbing her face in the sheets with a slow yawn.

"What are you doing up, Elijah?" Jordyn groaned. "And why are you just staring at me?"

"I wasn't," I said, looking at the nightstand on her side, reaching over to grab her phone. "I think I left my phone at my sister's house. I haven't had it all last night."

"Mmmm," was all she said as I went through her text messages. Fuck what y'all think when you reading this. Technically she wasn't my girlfriend, but I did care. I wanted to know who she was fucking, who else she was talking to, and whose ass I would eventually have to beat over her. The thought of her giving it up to another nigga always fucked with my head, but I never showed it. Bitches get caught up when they see a nigga slippin'. They either do some reckless shit like fuck around even more, or get clingy as hell. I didn't want Jordyn doing either. So, I always kept how I felt about her to myself, but truth be told, I was in love with her. I fell in love with her when she went the fuck off on me in that parking lot at the school. Shit, might have been when I first met her, when she didn't know who I was and didn't care to know. The sex only made my feelings for her stronger, and the fact that she's into girls? Shit, we got something in common off the top! But to protect my heart, my feelings, I would never tell her. Just wanted to keep her right where she was.

"What all you gotta do, baby?" I asked, scrolling through messages between her and some nigga named Rico. It was school-related shit.

"I have to buy groceries, and then rehearsal on the yard later on this afternoon." She yawned, turning over to look at me. I looked at her, sleepy gray eyes shining bright against her brown complexion. Her curly hair was all over the place, coming down past her ribs. That fucking hair. Damn. A bitch can be blind, deaf, and have one leg, but if that hair looking right? A nigga coming for it. Believe that. I love a woman with beautiful hair. A phat ass never hurt either, but that hair is what did it for me.

"I got to stop by my sister's house to find my phone. Think I left it in her room. And meet up with my manager, and see what the fuck we going to do about Jahiem crazy ass."

"What happened with him?"

"Got arrested over some fuck racist shit." I sighed, scratching my shoulder as I slowly got up, stretching, locs falling as I shook them freely out of my face. Only thing I had on was my gold chain. My body was covered in artwork, and I was planning on getting some more.

Setting her phone down on my dresser, I walked out, ready to greet my two dogs. My two bitches. Right now, I was loving my life. I had hit songs floating on the charts, niggas coming after us, trying to get us to sign with the big labels. We'd already made up our mind a while back we were going to stay independent, not fucking with that corporate shit on any level except on our own time and money. I was blessed with no kids, lived to see twenty-four, and all in all, I got the girl of my dreams sleeping in my bed with me.

After showering, getting dressed, and taking Jordyn out for breakfast, I dropped her off at the house. First stop was to see my manager, to try to work out the next few weeks. They were trying to get us featured onto so many damn songs, trying to get us to go worldwide and do festivals in different countries. Shit, I was down as the long as the money was right. I met up with the lawyer to see what the fuck we were going to do about that reckless-ass mothafucka Jahiem.

Then I had to see about my phone. I knew that shit was being blown up all damn night and morning. I had my work phone on me, so I was good without one phone for a while, but I knew I was missing a lot of my hoes' text messages and calls. So, with my bottle of water in hand, music blasting R Kelly, I made my way over to Olivia's house later on that evening. I was into old school R&B. That was my thing. A lot of people would assume the type of music I listen to is straight rap. Nah, bruh. I'd been singing since I could remember, and whatever my mama listened to, whether it was gospel, white pop shit, or R&B, I was right there with her, listening to it.

Shit, today was a good day, and it was going to be an even better night once we touched down in New York. Meeting up with Ontrell and Anthony during our meeting had me hype as fuck. Sunday was always a good day when I got to be with my brothers, man. Always some chaotic shit, but overall a good time when it was more than three Carters in a room.

Speaking of Carters, I smiled thinking about how Olivia had tried to play sick on our birthday.

I called her out on that bullshit of a lie last night. She had a boyfriend. I didn't know who, but I told her one way or another we were going to find out. Then I thought about Taylor, who probably fucked around with Trent last night. Let me find out his punk ass didn't hit it last night after she kept throwing him the signs.

Hopping out of the truck, feeling the cool evening air, I looked down at myself to make sure I was straight. Locs were pulled back, and I had on some comfortable-ass gray harem pants with the crotch low and Bart Simpson's face printed all over. That was my nigga from day one. I wore a black long-sleeve T-shirt, with a black jacket and matching yellow Future Flight J's. I was comfortable today. Wasn't trying to dress like I had money. *Shit, I am money, fuck that.*

I walked up to the door, doing a quick knock before stuffing my hands in the low pockets. The door swung open, and I saw Taylor's face looking shocked and almost terrified. She was standing in her red plaid pajama bottoms and oversized shirt, with her hair wrapped up, looking damn near like she had killed someone. She didn't want me to say shit about her and Trent. *I peeped it, shawty.*

"Aye, I just came—"

"Look, I don't know what you heard, but—"

"Nah, move out the way." I smirked, pushing the door aside as I stepped in, looking around. It looked like they were in the middle of cleaning up. *Yeah, I bet y'all hoe asses was cleaning up.*

Taylor grabbed my arm, standing in front of me like she didn't want me to go farther into the house. "What did Trent tell you?" she pressed as I smiled.

"I mean, what you all shook up for, shawty?" I asked. "Nigga told me everything," I lied, seeing if I could get her to spill everything. "I know about everything that happened here."

"Okay, so look, you realize that we are going to handle it ourselves. We don't need y'all interfering with this," she said, and my face scrunched up in confusion.

"Fuck is you talking about, Taylor?"

"What are you talking about?" she asked, backing up.

"Look, I came here to get my phone that I left in Olivia's room and to see if you and Trent got it on last night." I laughed, moving her out of the way.

"Oh my God. Okay, hold up! Trent didn't tell you?" she freaked, standing in front of me again, hands on my chest, looking terrified. "So, you don't know what happened? With him? Look, before you—"

I tuned her out, seeing Olivia walk out of the
bathroom. I caught a glimpse of the side of her
face, seeing it was swollen.

"Livie!" I called out, and she turned around,
eyes wide. Bruh! When I tell y'all reading this
shit, I damn near fell out at the sight of my sister's face. I moved Taylor out of the way, rushing
toward Olivia, and grabbed her arm as she tried
hiding her face, looking at the floor. "Look at
me! What the fuck happened?"

"Elijah, move!" she let out, voice cracking as I
grabbed her chin, making her wince in pain, but
fuck it. I had her eye level with my face, wanting
to know what happened.

"Who did this shit?" I asked in a low voice,
seeing her eyes water up. Her face was fucked up
beyond recognition. Her left cheek was purple
and red, eyes barely open, lip swollen, and
looking at her knuckles, I could see them shits
was bruised too. I couldn't breathe. I felt like
somebody fucked me up just as bad as they did
her. "Olivia!" I snapped. "Who did it?"

She wouldn't even look at me. I could feel my
eyes about to water up at the sight of my own
sister, my heart, a third of me, looking like this.

"Taylor, who the fuck did this?"

"Her boyfriend," Taylor mumbled, looking
down at the floor. "Trent and I were gone when

that happened, but we were here when they first started arguing, and Trent fought him. I thought everything was said and done. Trent wasn't trying to calm down, so I had to take him back, but when I got back . . ."

Her voice trailed off, and I looked at my sister again, seeing she was crying. Rarely has a nigga tried her to the point where all seven of us had to step in. Rarely. She was treated like royalty in these fucking streets. She was the only daughter, only female Carter, and was spoiled more than anyone. What nigga in his right mind thought he could get away with laying hands on my sister? Everyone in Atlanta knew who she was, because they knew me. You couldn't know her without knowing me, because we looked exactly alike. When they knew me, they knew Shiloh and Anthony. When they knew those looney-ass niggas, they knew our pops, who had pull in every fucking zone in Atlanta. So, whoever this nigga was had to be new to the city or something. Either way, he was about to get welcomed offi-cially.

I let her go without another word and went into her room, seeing my phone on the dresser where I'd left it. Fuck, bruh, I couldn't believe someone put their hands on my sister.

Sitting on the edge of the bed, I went through my phone, seeing Trent had texted me, telling me what had happened. All I saw was the word *rape*, and I immediately called Olivia in the room. Both Taylor and Olivia stood in the doorway, and it took all I had not to cry like a bitch to see my sister like that.

"He was about to rape you?" I asked.

"No! That's Trent's stupid-ass, made-up story! Navier wouldn't do that to me!"

"Look at yo' fucking face!" I shouted, not at all shocked by her naïve mind. "Bruh, don't even worry about it though, Livie. You sticking up for this nigga; I hope you say a prayer for him too," I mumbled, calling Anthony.

"Hello?" he answered, and I heard my nieces and nephews in the background. "Aye! Sit y'all bad asses down and wait for her to bring the plate to you!"

"Aye, hold up, bruh. Let me call Shiloh and put him on," I said. "Call Trell and tell him to call Trent. Hold up real quick. This is an emergency."

"Shit, a'ight," he said as I clicked over, dialing Shiloh's number.

"Y'all are overreacting and being so fucking dramatic about—"

"Shut the fuck up, Olivia," I snapped, and she stormed out of the room. I was waiting for

Shiloh to pick up as I clicked back over. Taylor went after her friend, and I got up to close the door, locking it.

"What's good?" Shiloh answered coolly just as Trell got on the phone with Trent.

"Yo, Trent, get Talin on the phone, nigga," I demanded.

"I'm already on the phone. What the fuck is going on? I ain't never talked to this many niggas on the phone before like this," Talin snapped.

"This is gay as fuck, though," Anthony mumbled. "Trell, you be doing shit like this?"

"Shut the fuck up," Ontrell snapped, and they laughed.

I was about to cut the noise real quick. "So, look, Olivia got her ass beat by her boyfriend last night," I stated, hearing everyone go silent. Trent was the first to speak.

"I was there. He didn't—"

"Nigga, you left, bruh!" I snapped at Trent. "After you left, this nigga went the fuck in on her face! All of y'all need to get over here ASAP."

"Say no more," Anthony said, and everyone hung up at the same time.

Stepping back out into the living room, I could see Olivia was sitting on the couch, crying, with Taylor holding her.

"You need to ice yo' face," I told her, sitting on the other couch.

She popped her head up to look at me, angrier at me than the nigga who beat her face in.

"Don't talk to me, Elijah—"

"No, I'm going to keep talking to you, Olivia," I snapped, getting up. "You always get away with the dumbest shit, but to let this nigga beat yo'—"

"I didn't let him! I fought back! I told him to get off me, and I told him—"

"I don't want to hear it," I said, hand up. I didn't want to even imagine my sister struggling, not underneath a nigga, not financially, nor physically, emotionally, none of that. I got up, and Taylor moved out of the way. I wrapped my arms around Olivia, who started crying on my shoulder. I was feeling everything she was feeling: hurt, anger, and pain. I felt it. When you are born a twin, or triplet or whatever, it's a bond that is stronger than just yo' basic brother and sister. Our mama always said when one of us fell, the other cried. If one of us got a shot at the doctor, especially if it was Trent because that nigga stayed sick as a kid, I was the one that cried for him like I got the shot. Never failed.

Suddenly, there was a hard knock on the door, and Taylor quickly went to open it. In walked Anthony, big Rick-Ross-with-dreads mothafucka, with Ontrell and Talin behind him. As soon as they got a look at her face, they were on the same heated level that I was on.

"So, who the fuck is this nigga?" Anthony asked, grabbing her jaw to examine her face more closely.

"Do it matter?" Ontrell snapped.

"Shit, let me get a name before we put the nigga to sleep, bruh." Anthony laughed sarcastically as the door pushed open again. Trent walked in, and I could tell he had been in a fight. His face had a scratch and his lip was red, but that was it. Nigga would protect that face at all costs. Knowing him, the pretty nigga didn't fight to defend himself. He threw hands to keep that face. *SMH*.

"So, what happened?" Talin asked, crossing his arms over his chest as he looked at Trent and Taylor.

We stood there in her living room, listening to Trent and Taylor tell the story. All of us were brown-skin to dark with locs, except for Trent, who stood out as always with his light complexion and low haircut. If Jahiem was there, he would have been right there along with his yellow ass. Shit, he should have been there. We were always separated into two groups: the hard-headed ones and the common-sense niggas. Jahiem, Trell, and I fought on sight. Drop of a dime, we were ready to fight anyone and everybody. We'd ask questions later—or never.

Trent, Shiloh, Talin, and Anthony were calm as fuck about it. They only fought when they had to. Anthony and Talin were family niggas. Shiloh had people that would fight for him on command, and Trent was too pretty to get his hands dirty. Simple shit.

"Where the fuck were you when all this was going down?" Ontrell asked, sounding like a straight bitch.

"I told you I was with her!" Trent snapped, pointing at Taylor. "We were in the room, woke up, and heard Olivia yelling. I didn't hear the nigga until she screamed out. As soon as I went in there, I went off on dude. It ain't like I sat here and did nothing! Olivia put me out her room, locked herself in there with that nigga."

Anthony went off. "But why you ain't say shit? You could have called us. We could have been came over here and handled this."

"If y'all would have saw how Olivia was acting, you would know she didn't even want me here. She wanted to be grown—"

"Not a matter of being grown, Trent!" Olivia snapped, and I cut my eyes at her. This shit started a whole new argument. Olivia was good for flip-flopping like hell. When the blame started to be put on her, she would blink those hazel eyes and play victim until someone fell for it.

"Stop talking to me, Livie. Just shut the fuck up," Trent said slowly, shaking his head.

"Don't tell me to shut—"

"A'ight so now we need to find out where he's at, who he roll with, and what the fuck he getting into tonight," Anthony plotted, cutting in between the two while grabbing his keys. "Anyone associated with that nigga when we get a hold of him is getting it."

"Y'all don't have to go out and hurt anyone! Why are y'all even taking—"

The door opened, and Shiloh stepped in, bringing in the cold before closing it shut. He looked like he just woke up, wearing sweats, a hoodie, and a jean jacket. With everyone going back and forth on how to handle this shit, Shiloh took one look at Olivia and shook his head, jaw tightening up.

"Nah," he let out slowly, shaking his head. He was a man of few words, but his look said it all.

"Find out where he at, Livie," Anthony demanded.

When she refused, being the spoiled brat that she was, he took the phone from her and had Taylor text this nigga. Everyone was going off on each other in this small-ass living room, talking about what we should do, what we were not doing, what we could do. Shiloh stayed quiet, keeping his eyes on Olivia. Trent was still in his feelings, so he didn't even look her way, and Trell, who was the youngest, ran his mouth like he was about that life. Every fucking Sunday when we got together, it was on some chaotic bullshit.

"Aye, listen! Listen!" Taylor shouted out, standing on top of the couch with her hand held up to get everyone's attention. She looked at the phone, scrolling through. "So, he texted back saying he's at some nigga's house named Lee for the night. Do you know where that is?"

Olivia nodded.

"Let's go," Shiloh said, opening the front door. "Olivia, get in the car with me."

We all walked out of the small house, with Taylor slipping on her coat and shoes.

"You riding with me or yo' boyfriend?" I asked her with a smirk.

She rolled her eyes at me. "Nigga, shut up," she retorted as she got in the truck with me on the passenger's side. Trent decided last-minute to get in the truck, sitting in the back, and we pulled out, falling behind Shiloh and Livie.

"I can't believe she let that nigga beat on her," Taylor mumbled. "And I wasn't here to stop it."

"He probably would've got yo' ass too, Big Tay," I joked, looking in the rearview mirror at Trent, who kept quiet. "Y'all were too busy fucking, though."

"Shut the fuck up, Elijah!" Trent snapped, hitting me hard in the back of the head. I turned around so quick, trying to hit him in that pretty little face.

"Would both of y'all stop?" Taylor cried out, grabbing the steering wheel as I turned back around. "Y'all act like fucking kids sometimes. Yo' sister was beaten badly by another nigga, and y'all sitting here talking about who fucked who?" We grew quiet, and I glanced at Taylor. "Nigga, what?"

"Sounds like the sex wasn't all that great," I mumbled, and they both hit me, causing me to laugh.

We ended up going all the way on the south side of Atlanta, pulling up to a dark street with the streetlights barely lit. Small houses lined up on either side, and we pulled up alongside the curb to the one on the corner. All the jokes and laughing came to a stop immediately when I got out. You really about to see how we get down, reader. Put away the jokes, the music, the money, everything. All that shit goes out the window when it comes to our own.

"Aye," I said, watching Trell tie up his locks. We all stood on the yard, with Shiloh talking to Olivia, who sat in the car. "What's the Spanish nigga name again?"

"Jose or some shit," Talin answered, tying his locs up.

"Navier," Anthony answered, trying not to laugh. "Aye, Talin and Trent, grab the phones. Don't let nobody out this fucking house; don't let nobody in."

We walked up to the door as I peeped two more cars pull up and park on the side of the house. Shiloh had his niggas watching the whole area.

"Lemme knock," Trell said eagerly, and I scrunched my face, moving out of the way so he could ring the doorbell.

"Well, then knock with yo' punk ass. Damn," I retorted.

We looked like six niggas politely asking to invade somebody's house. But we are the Carter Boys, not fucking low-life criminals. I like to think we can be classy about this shit, you feel me?

Trell banged hard on the door three times, and then rang the doorbell back to back, letting these niggas know it was a problem before they even opened the door.

"Who is it?" someone called out.

"Open the fucking door, bruh. Don't worry about who it is!" Anthony snapped, tying his locs down. Mine could stay loose. I watched Shiloh walk toward us after talking with Olivia, looking at me.

"Nobody move until I do," he stated. "E, you with me."

"Yeah," I said with no hesitation. Like I said, while Trent was busy busting his ass in school, I was rolling with Shiloh everywhere. Can't say I regret missing out on school and learning something, but if I could do it all over again, I would have kept my black ass in school with that nigga.

"Grandma, I don't know who it is," the boy said, and Trent cut his eyes at me, wide. I barely blinked.

The door opened, and there stood this short little older lady, with her glasses, long pink nightgown on, thin gray hair in small curls that were looking church ready, and a cigarette in hand.

"What in Jesus' name? Who are y'all, and what—"

"Is Navier here?" Anthony asked as we moved closer.

I could see two girls sitting on the couch, and two younger boys standing behind the lady, looking at us. The smell of cooked food came pouring out of the house as the TV blared MTV.

"Navier is downstairs in the basement with—"

Shiloh made his way in between us, and without so much as a word, grabbed the lady by her hair, gripping hard. He pushed her against the table, causing her to fall back to the floor, while the rest of us stepped inside, closing and locking the door.

The Reveal

Noelle

"I will be sure to stop by, Aunt Alice," I said, placing my hand on top of her small, dainty hand. I was in the process of leaving church when one of the older ladies stopped me with her grandkids in tow, inviting me over for dinner. I knew she was trying to set me up with her grandson, but I know she wanted some company as well.

"Make sure you bring your best dish, honey," she said, patting down her tiny gray curls in her hair before pushing up her glasses. "You know men love it when you can cook."

"Oh, I know." I smiled, thinking about Shiloh. I felt a hand on my back, and I looked back, seeing one of the guys from the choir smiling hard at me.

"Hey, wanted to catch you on your way out, Noelle," Michael said as Aunt Alice cheesed at me.

"Mm-hmm, you better walk her to her car, young man, if you trying to get with her," she said, and I laughed, dropping my head in shame. Never go to a small church where everyone notices you the moment you arrive. I was the new girl here, and I was constantly being set up with grandson after grandson, no matter how many times I told them I had a boyfriend.

"I'll be sure to do that, ma'am." Michael smiled politely back, and we watched her walk out with her grandkids.

I looked up at him, and we both started cracking up with a shake of our heads. Michael was a handsome black man, light brown complexion, low-cut hair, perfect teeth, tall, and always polite. He was a personal trainer by profession, but I would catch him here on Sundays, singing with the choir. He was a nice-looking man, perfect for me if I really thought about it. Yet, there was Shiloh. . . .

"Have any clients today?" I asked, maneuvering our way through the packed crowd, trying to leave the church.

"You know I do. Always working," he said, hand on my lower back, guiding me.

I wore my cute red Ralph Lauren black label dress, my Rachel Roy long trench coat with the fur on the hood, and matching heels. My hair trimmed and down, with a small curl at the end. I knew the congregation would joke around, calling Michael and me the Barbie and Ken of the church because we took pride in how we looked, but honestly, I was starting to get uncomfortable with how people kept pinning us together.

After saying goodbye to everyone, we stood outside as I looked around for Shiloh, who was supposed to pick me up and take me on a lunch date.

"You didn't drive today?" Michael asked, taking out his keys as he put on his coat. It was definitely a cold Sunday morning. The sun was barely out, and crackled-up leaves rolled up on the pavement as the wind whipped.

"Not today. My boyfriend is supposed to take me on a date." I smiled, and he dropped his head. "What was that for?" I laughed.

"Bye, y'all two!" Miss Mavis waved. With Michael's hand on my back, we waved back, watching her step into the parking lot.

"Don't forget, Noelle, you stopping by tonight!" Aunt Alice called out. "I want you to meet Lee!"

"I hear ya." I smiled, waving at her before turning to Michael with a dull look on my face as he laughed. "You see what I have to put up with?

I tell people I have a boyfriend, and nobody wants to listen."

"You're too beautiful to have a boyfriend. That's why," he joked.

"That doesn't even make sense, Michael."

"I'm saying,"—he shrugged—"either men are going to wish they were with you, or try to get with you. You got all these little ol' ladies wanting to set you up because you dang near perfect."

"Awww," I cooed, and we both started laughing. "That was sweet."

"It's the truth," he mumbled, looking at his keys. "So, where is this so-called boyfriend you keep throwing in our faces?"

"Uhh, well," I mumbled, looking around the parking lot. The moment I spotted that Mustang pull into the lot, I smiled, and pointed. "He's coming." Looking at Michael, I could see his eyes stayed on me.

"Hope your dude is secure in himself, because there are a lot of guys that would do anything to be with you," he said, and I smirked with a roll of my eyes.

"Yeah, right."

"Okay." He shrugged, hands in the air as we laughed. "Just a fair warning to all the crazies out there. Hope your guy can handle it."

Watching Shiloh's Mustang pull up with that loud engine, blasting Kendrick Lamar, I smiled. He was definitely turning heads as the congregation continued to pour out into the parking lot.

"I have to go. I'll see you next Sunday?" I asked, arms out as we hugged, careful to keep it short and simple.

"Of course," Michael said, hand lingering on my lower back as I quickly pulled away. He turned to walk back in the church, greeting people on his way inside.

I walked toward car, getting in and feeling the warmth take over before closing the door.

"Oooh, it's soo cold," I let out, rubbing my hands together as I looked at Shiloh, who stared at me with no smile, no expression, nothing. He was wearing gray harem pants, a hoodie, and a jean jacket, like he'd just rolled out of bed, with black Jordans on. His low black curly hair was tamed, and those low-lid eyes shifted to the direction in front of him, moving forward with the car.

"Why aren't you dressed for our date?" I pressed, slipping my seatbelt on.

"I just woke up not too long ago," he answered coolly. "Who is that nigga you were talking to?"

"Michael?" I asked with a smile. "He's a part of the choir at the church. Ugh, you won't believe how many people constantly keep trying to hook us up, even after I tell them I have a boyfriend. They call him Ken and me Barbie. That's our nicknames. Can you believe that?" I laughed with a shake of my head.

He said nothing, just kept driving, occasionally glancing out the window as he leaned back in his seat, one hand on the steering wheel.

"We were actually talking about you when you pulled up."

"Oh, yeah?" he said in a quiet tone.

"Mm-hmm. He was telling me he hopes my boyfriend is secure in himself because apparently a lot of guys would do anything to be with me, or something like that," I rambled on. I knew exactly what Michael said. I just wanted to see what Shiloh's reaction would be. I wanted to know if he was the jealous or territorial type of man.

"I bet," was all he said.

I just smiled. I don't know why I was expecting some big, dramatic scene from Shiloh. We rode in silence, listening to music, with him occasionally asking me how was church. He was attempting to make conversation, which I appreciated, knowing he wasn't the talking type.

When we made it to his place, he told me he was going to shower and change before we stepped back out. So, I kicked my heels off, coat laying in the living room, as I sat on his bed, hearing the shower running in the bathroom. Smirking, I thought about what he could look like naked. I'd never seen him naked in the light before. Usually when he spent the night, he had on basketball shorts, and it was dark, so I couldn't see much. For once, I wanted to wipe that dry, dull, stone expression off his face and replace it with shock, surprise, maybe even anger. It was almost like I was testing him out, seeing how far I could go with him before knowing when to back down.

I got up, tying my hair up in a bun, slipping my tights off as I walked toward the bathroom door and slowly pushed it open. I could barely see anything with the steam in the air as I peeked at the black curtains. I walked in, careful not to make a sound as I closed the door behind me, trying so hard not to laugh. I could have sworn I heard him singing, but I wasn't sure. I imagined him standing there like a rock, just washing himself, staring at the corner of the tub. Yet, the moment I heard him humming, almost singing, I could barely contain my laughter. Oh yeah, now I definitely wanted to surprise him. He wasn't going to be expecting this.

Sex was never a topic between us. He never tried me sexually, and he barely kissed me on the mouth. It was always a hug, simple kiss on the cheek, and nothing more. So, I knew the risk I was taking when I decided to do this. Slipping out of my red dress, I stood there in my white lingerie, push-up lace bra, and matching boy shorts against my dark complexion. Moving closer, I put my hand on the small sink, accidentally knocking his small bottle of oil to the floor. Shit! I froze as the water and humming came to a stop.

"I know you in here, Noelle," was all he said as my face dropped, body becoming relaxed in defeat.

"You sing in the shower, Shiloh?" I asked teasingly as he pulled the curtains back.

Sweet baby Jesus, I nearly fainted at the sight of this man. My man. He looked at me, definitely on hard, before stepping out of the tub. His light caramel complexion was soaked, with that wet, short, black curly hair dripping onto his face. His body was indescribable; V cut leading to . . . I quickly looked away in embarrassment.

"I'm so sorry." I laughed, covering my eyes.

"I was only humming to keep you in here. I could see you through the mirror when you first came in," he said, walking toward me.

I backed up so quick, body hitting the closed door, until he stood in front of me. I almost forgot I was standing there naked in my panties, until I glanced at him, seeing his tongue was already halfway out his mouth, eyes traveling on slow-mo over my body.

"Shiloh," I let out, feeling him move closer, feeling his thing hit my leg. "Oh my God, Shiloh, I didn't mean to come in here. I was just kidding!" I laughed nervously, looking up at the ceiling, avoiding his gaze. "If you want me to leave, I can go, because this isn't my bathroom. I didn't mean to—"

He leaned down and kissed me on the lips, shutting me up quick, while pulling my body close to his. It was like everything he wanted to say to me when he was around me, he let it out through this kiss. I don't know what happened, but everything became silent, my body was numb, and I began breathing deeper as I followed his lead, letting him take control. My hands? I don't even know what the hell they were doing, just pressed against my stomach, scared to touch his body. This wasn't supposed to happen. I was supposed to surprise him, catch him off guard, not the other way around.

When he pulled back, he let out a hard sigh. "Can I get dressed, please?" he asked simply, looking away.

I glanced down at this thing, seeing he was throbbing, veins popping out in every direction. I smirked as I looked up at him.

"Are you really getting dressed, or something else?" I asked, and he looked at me, tiniest hint of a smile at the corners of his mouth. It was all I could ask for in a day. If I could get him to smile once, I would be happy.

"I'm not answering that, Noelle," was all he said, and I let out a huge laugh, turning to open the door. Men are so easy and simple; disgusting, yet addicting.

"I'll leave you to it, then," I cheesed, walking out.

When he came out, halfway dressed with another pair of gray low-crotch sweats, this time a darker color showing off his boxers, he immediately got on the phone to talk about plans for the night. I sat on his bed, still undressed, as I listened, watching him go in and out of his closet, shirtless.

Today was supposed to be the day Tyree got the rest of his stuff out of his apartment. I honestly hoped the best for him, but I couldn't afford to have someone else stay with me. I did the whole roommate thing, and I wasn't really a fan of it.

"Yeah, we can hit him up tonight then, bruh," Shiloh said, walking out of the closet as he looked at me. "Yeah, a'ight." Hanging up, he tossed the phone on the bed next to me.

"Hit what up?" I asked curiously, watching his eyes look me over. I knew exactly what I was doing, and I didn't plan on stopping. The biggest tease in the world might be me. I'm pretty sure I've teased more men than anyone. It was fun for me to see a moment of weakness in their face, especially Shiloh, who displayed anything but weakness until it came to me.

"Can you put yo' clothes on?" he asked softly.

I shook my head, smirking. Lying back on the bed, I stretched with an obnoxious yawn, legs reaching toward the ceiling before falling lazily open back on the bed. This was so much better than a simple lunch date where I would do all the talking and he would listen. Way better.

I looked down, seeing him stare at me. Oh, this was too funny.

"Today is such a beautiful lousy day. I don't feel like doing anything." I sighed, turning over on my stomach, facing the headboard. His bed felt like he hadn't slept in it for days or weeks. It was made up to perfection.

"You think you funny, Noelle," he mumbled as I laughed, rolling on my back once more.

"What am I doing?"

"You fucking with a nigga. The wrong nigga. That's what you're doing," he stated, voice serious as my smile dropped. "Please don't do that. If I'm patiently waiting for you to give me your body, don't throw that shit in my face because you know I won't do nothing. I'm respecting you. I want the same in return. Period," was all he said.

"I was just playing, Shiloh," I mumbled, grabbing my dress. My mood had officially been killed. "You don't have to get all mad about it."

"I'm not mad," he said, sitting on the edge of the bed, watching me slide my dress on once again.

"Well, you have a tone," I retorted, feeling combative.

He tilted his head to the side, looking at me. "What's wrong with you, shawty? Why you trying to bait me into arguing with you, sneaking into my bathroom, doing all this teasing fuck shit in my bed? Nigga at the church, relaying some bullshit he said about me. What's the problem? You on your period or something?"

he asked bluntly as my mouth dropped, looking at him.

"I'm just trying to get an emotion or something out of you," I said. I could have snapped on him right there, but it wasn't worth it. "You're always so cold and distant. I just . . . I don't know how to talk to you. How do I know if you really even like me if you don't act like it?"

He said nothing. I got up to stand in front of him so he could get the zipper.

"Can you zip this, please?"

He stood up close behind me, taking the zipper in his hand before I continued on.

"I mean, I just don't get you. How is it when I first moved here, I saw you with girls, kissing on them, walking them to their car, talking whatever; yet, when you get to me, it's nothing? I am a woman. I like affection. I like a show of dominance," I said, feeling the dress being zipped up. I turned around and looked him directly in his eye. "I would like to know that my guy likes me enough to recognize when another guy is pushing up on me. Or, if I get undressed in front of him, to know that I feel sexy. That I can make a man weak just by looking at me. Sometimes I crack jokes, and you never laugh. Sometimes I do shit to piss you off purposely, and you never say a word. Don't even blink. I am a woman, Shiloh, your woman," I cooed, grabbing him by both arms to playfully shake him as his eyes never left mine. "Make me feel like you actually give a fuck about me. You telling me to put my clothes back on is not the move, boo," I said with a small smile.

His face stayed the exact same. I could have poured my soul out, I could be dying, and he wouldn't care. I pulled away, about to look for my shoes, when he grabbed my arm to pull me back toward him.

"What do you want, robot?" I pressed, looking up at him with a dull look.

He dropped his head with a sigh, hands coming to my waist as we stood close, bodies touching against each other.

"I like you, Noelle. I look forward to seeing you get in yo' car every morning, rushing to yo' job because you stay being late as fuck. And every morning, you drop that fucking phone, and I can hear you cussing out loud," he said, and I laughed. That fucking phone dropped in the same spot every damn morning. "I like when you be in the kitchen going off on me because I bring food over without asking you and expect you to cook for me. You do it anyway, and I appreciate that. When you sleep, I have to wake up in the middle of the night to keep you from falling off the bed because you stay moving. When you sing in the shower, but if you fuck up on the song, you start over. Shit gets me every time, because you never finish an entire song; or when you talk about sports, sounding like the typical female who thinks they know what the fuck they talking about."

"I do!" I shrieked, and he smiled. A true smile.

"I'm not yo' typical nigga that you're used to dealing with," he said in a serious voice, gazing hard at me. "Me being quiet and chill is how I've always been. That will never change, because talking makes me uncomfortable. I'm most happy and relaxed when I'm chill. Don't take it as me not wanting you, or not liking you, because you are the only thing that is a constant in my mind," he said fiercely, and my heart started to flutter.

I just nodded, feeling like a wimp, ready to break out the tears of happiness like in the movies when someone finally declares their love for someone.

"I will never raise my voice at you, never disrespect you, and my loyalty is only to you. I expect the same in return. You getting mad at me is going to happen, because you're a female. Y'all emotional like that, but I will never show that side of me to you."

"I'm going to have to see it someday, though," I reasoned as he shook his head.

"You'll never see it unless you fuck with my family, my money, and trust," he warned as I took a deep swallow. "That goes for anyone. Those are the three things I hold close to me." He grew quiet, just watching me. I slowly smiled.

"So, you do like me?" I asked softly.

He smirked, wrapping his arms around my neck to bring me close to his bare chest as I laughed. "I like you, Noelle," he said, kissing the side of my face. I felt like a milestone had been reached between the two of us. "I keep my distance from you physically because I want you and that chocolate body in every way possible, but you not trying to give a nigga none," he said.

I laughed, pulling away from him. "Well, people are willing to do crazy things for this body, apparently, so I can understand your frustration," I retorted, and he rolled his eyes. It was the first time I'd ever seen him do that!

"Tell that Barbie-doll nigga at yo' church to try that shit if he want to. Better be glad I didn't see his face. Find out real quick just how secure the fuck I am," he stated, walking back to his bathroom, pulling his sweats up, expression on his face blank as usual. No smile, nothing.

I smiled, watching him grab his keys and slip on a shirt with a hoodie. That was all I wanted to hear.

Of course, we went out to eat for our date. I wanted seafood, but he was allergic to it, so we opted for Italian, which he'd never had before. I nearly slapped him when he said he never had Italian food before. All those damn pastas I made for him since he loved to eat it, but he never had real Italian food? He needed to step out of the hood and live a little. I always told him that.

I ate light since I was heading over to Aunt Alice's house that night, just to be friendly, grab a plate for Shiloh, who wanted some, and leave. So, later on in the evening, with Tyree being out of the house all day, I quickly dressed down into something a bit more comfortable: jeans, black riding boots, cute peach-colored top, and light accessories. Nothing fancy. I didn't want to impress anyone, but never would I look like a slob outside of my house.

Grabbing my coat, I stepped out, seeing it was starting to get dark when I heard my phone ring.

"Hello?" I answered with a smile as I got in the car.

"Aye," Shiloh greeted in his usual dull demeanor. "When you go over there, see if you can slip like—"

"Get four plates!" I heard his friend Jaeden yell out. "I want some!"

"Nah, get me one too!" I could hear Semaj call out.

Yes, I knew a couple of his friends on a first-name basis.

"Get out my fucking ear, bruh!" Shiloh snapped angrily before flipping the script, coming at me with the calmest voice. "Get what you can get, Noe," he said, calling me by the nickname he gave me a couple of days ago. "You know where I'll be at."

"Are you spending the night with me?" I asked, trying to follow the directions on the GPS screen prompted on my dashboard, courtesy of Shiloh. Aunt Alice wasn't far, but there was a lot of turning and streets I had to keep switching on if I wanted to avoid the highways.

"Is Tyree spending the night?"

I smiled, knowing he didn't like him being at my house any more than I did, even if it was just the weekend.

"I haven't seen him all day, so I'm not sure."

He grew quiet, and I sighed.

"He's your brother's boyfriend. I don't know why you have a problem—"

"Hold up. This is my brother calling me," he said before the phone went silent.

Setting the phone in my lap on speaker, I continued to follow the directions until I reached the neighborhood. Looking down at my phone, I saw the call had ended. He would realize it and call me back, I thought.

Pulling up to her house on the corner, I decided to park on the side, since I didn't plan on staying long. This definitely reminded me of home in Albany with my own grandma. Stepping out, I closed the door just as her front door opened. I immediately smelled good, homemade cooking float in the air as I quickly made my way inside. She had a house full.

"I'm glad you didn't bring that Michael with you," she teased as I bent down to hug her small frame. She stood in her pink nightgown, hair still in its small, thin curls, and wide, gold-rimmed glasses taking up most of her face. I could smell the cigarette smoke on her, but could smell other type of smoke coming from below.

"I thought you liked Michael," I said, shocked she would even say that—or think I would bring him in the first place.

"Something ain't right with that boy," she said, shaking her head as she directed me toward the kitchen. "You didn't bring a dish, I see."

"I brought some drinks, though," I cheesed, holding up the bags I got from the grocery store earlier with Shiloh. Her typical grand-kids were running around, with the two teenage girls sitting on the couch, watching music videos back to back. I remember that age, looking at the screen, wanting to wear every-thing I saw the cool girls wearing on TV. I thought showing skin was being sexy and cute. Now I knew: not always, and definitely not all the time.

So, I made myself comfortable in her kitchen, helping her with the chicken and collard greens. She was definitely making some soul food today.

"Hold up. Let me call the boys up here," she said as she patted me on the back like she was excited for me. "June! Go git' them boys up here now."

"Yes, ma'am," the girl said as she quickly walked down to the basement. Aunt Alice smiled at me. "Now, only one I want you paying atten-tion to is my grandson Leeroy, or Lee. The rest are his little friends."

"How old are these boys?" I pressed, wondering if she knew I was older than I looked.

"They are mid twenties, same as you." She smiled knowingly. "I just need my son out this damn house and on his own, and it's going to take a girl to get him there."

"Oh Lord." I sighed with a smile. I could hear the rumble of footsteps as a door opened.

"Grandma, I told you not to be setting me up like this!" Lee complained as they turned the corner into the kitchen.

All four guys stood tall, looking like they were having an overgrown sleepover in basketball shorts, sweats, and raggedy white tank tops. The one called Lee was probably no bigger than a pencil, tall and lanky, with an awkward stance. The other three had a little weight to them, but stood just as awkwardly as he did.

"Hi." I smiled, and they all grinned.

"See? Didn't yo' grandma tell you she was gorgeous? You need to put some damn clothes on, running around this house looking like that and you got company!" Aunt Alice snapped as I tried to keep from laughing. "Go on and clean up down there so you can invite her down to the basement properly."

"Grandma—"

"Ehh! Boy, did I ask you a question, or did I just fucking tell you to do something?" she snapped.

Lee looked at me, mouthing *sorry*, and I shook my head, waving it off. Neither one of us wanted this to happen.

They went back down to the basement as I continued with the cooking, occasionally seeing the two teenage girls look at me from the couch. The little boys stayed running in and out of the kitchen, trying to mess with me, but I put an end to it quick, threatening that they wouldn't get a plate. Can't mess with a man about his food, no matter the age.

"You know Miss Faye at the church?" Aunt Alice started, getting into her gossiping stance as she leaned on the counter, legs crossed over each other, arms crossed over her chest.

"I do."

"Gurrl, lemme tell you what she said about our pastor," she started. "Talking about he's messing around on his wife. I said, girl, if you don't stop fooling around with these little rumors, it's gon' come and bite you back in the ass."

"Amen." I smiled, checking the chicken in the oven. "Just like how everyone keeps putting me with Michael."

"Honey, that man is obsessed with you. Anyone can see it. I don't trust it. Anyone that handsome, with his life together, and decent education, but you can't find a woman? Chile, something ain't right," she stated, shaking her head just as there was a serious banging noise on the front door, followed by the doorbell being rung at a rapid rate. "What in the—Li'l Ray, go answer the damn door! I hope they know what the fuck time it is," Alice muttered, walking out of the kitchen.

I stayed put, turning around to the stove to check the rice, already calculating what I was putting on the plates to go. She had enough to feed a homeless shelter, so I was sure she wouldn't mind me taking a couple home. I definitely planned on teaching Shiloh how to cook one day. He—

"Grandma!" I heard one of the girls cry out in fear, and I quickly turned around, seeing her grandsons rush over to the couch, looking terrified. Before I could even react, I caught a glimpse of multiple bodies moving quickly throughout the house, hearing voices and commands.

"Yo, he's down here!" I heard one yell out just as this tall, brown-skin guy with short dreads, wearing all black, came in the kitchen, smirking at me.

"Bruh! I found me a pretty bitch in here!" he shouted.

My heart was beating so fast, body numb in panic, and I could barely breathe. As I started looking around for my phone, he shook his head, smiling.

"Nah, baby, you not calling nobody," he said, moving closer to me.

Right when I was about to let out a scream for help, he quickly grabbed me, disgusting hand covering my mouth tight as he licked my neck. I screamed, trying to kick and shake free of his tight grip.

"Shit, you taste good, too, looking like fucking chocolate ice cream. Damn." He breathed against my neck before biting it hard.

I could feel tears coming down as I tried my hardest to get out of his grasp, with him dragging me out of the kitchen. I could see Aunt Alice passed out on the floor, her grandkids in tears, clinging onto each other.

"Trell, what the fuck are you doing with her?" one of the others, who had a gun in his hand, asked.

"I'm about to fuck the shit out of her. This might be that fuck nigga's sister for all we know," he said as I quickly tried to fight back. "Hold her wild ass down."

I bit his hand, but he only held my mouth down tighter, other hand undoing my jeans as he pushed me hard up against the wall.

"Bruh, this is too fucking much for me," another said, sounding scared out of his mind. He was the only one with sense, while the rest carried on like animals.

"I said I was sorry! I told her I was sorry!" I heard someone yell as the basement door flew open, almost hitting us in the process. One of Lee's friends was gripped hard on the back of the neck by someone who had a gun in his hand.

"Nigga, we don't know what the fuck sorry means!" the guy yelled, slamming him hard into the floor as I cried out.

"Aye, he got a sister? A fine-ass chocolate sister?" the guy holding me asked with a laugh as another dread-head came up from the basement, dark-skin and smirking at us.

"Nigga, you already know I'm hitting it first!" He laughed, grabbing my hair, jerking my head to the side hard as I cried, feeling them shove their hands between my legs, gripping hard through the jeans.

"I don't know what else you want me to do!" the guy cried.

I heard something like a thud go off, seeing the guy bash Lee's head hard into the wall.

"That's our fucking sister! My sister!" the guy screamed again before they all went in on him.

"Yo, let's take her to the room," one of the guys said, still gripping my hair as he licked his lips at me. Tattoos were covering his entire neck, and some on his face.

"You want that?" the one who had his hand over my mouth asked, rubbing up against me aggressively. They both laughed, while I just closed my eyes, praying. All I could do at this point was pray.

"Aye! Let her go. She's not related to him," another said, and I opened my eyes, seeing Lee's friend wasn't moving. He was barely breathing. His face was covered with pure blood gushing out from every direction. The one who was doing all the yelling let out the biggest spitball on his face before kicking him again.

"He's still alive though, bruh," he said casually, in a dull-like voice. I knew that voice. I'd heard it before.

"Let him live, man."

"Nah! That nigga needs to be done with!" the one who had my hair said as he went over to the lifeless body and pulled out a gun, aiming it at him.

"So, what we going to do about the kids?" the one holding my mouth said.

"Clean 'em all out," the one with the dreads and gun said, aiming it at the kids as I shrieked from behind his hand. Everyone's eyes went to me, and it was in that second that my eyes locked with the last person I expected to be there.

Shiloh.

My heart was pounding so bad, body sweating and hands shaking through this whole experience, but seeing him made it all stop. It made me become numb to this hell, knowing he was a part of it. His face showed a brief flash of fear, with his eyes lighting up before he went completely brick cold, turning his attention back to the guy on the floor. I was just kissing this man, this fucking monster, a few hours ago. I let him sleep in the same bed as me! This couldn't be the same quiet, softspoken man I knew him to be when he was with me. No, this was someone different.

Suddenly, Lee's friend let out a groan in pain as he started to move his body to turn over on his stomach. Without hesitating, Shiloh quickly pulled out his gun and took the safety off. It caused me to shriek again behind the guy's hand, tears pouring over his fingers. I'd never been this scared before in my life. I could barely handle scary movies, let alone this shit right here.

He looked up at me, gun still cocked, almost like he was confused about what to do as he stared hard at me.

"Nah, let that nigga live. You just got out. Why the fuck you trying to get put back in for good?" another asked.

Shiloh kept his eyes only on me before slipping his gun behind him. "Aye," he said, bending down to Lee's friend to look him in the face. "You see that girl right there?" he said, pointing at me. "She's the one that just saved yo' mothafucking life!" he spat before shoving his foot so hard in the guy's neck the man starting coughing up blood, crying, his teeth and mouth oozing red.

"You tried to rape my sister and thought you could fucking get away with that shit!" Shiloh screamed, kicking him again. "If I catch you on these streets, you not gonna have her"—he pointed at me again—"to save you again! Might as well kill yo' own damn self, because you not gonna last three days in Atlanta. Know this," he ended, spitting on him again before walking out. "Let's go."

I watching the guys pour out as the guy who held onto me backed up with confusion on his face, looking hard at me, like I was suddenly worth something—worth not messing with.

"How you know my brother?" he asked before someone called his name, telling him to come on.

I couldn't move. My body was trembling as I looked at the kids through watery eyes. When I felt it was safe to move, I quickly went to the kids, who were crying uncontrollably. Then I checked the basement, seeing his other friends were beaten just as badly. I needed to call the police, the ambulance, somebody.

To Be Continued . . .

Coming November 2018:

The Carter Boys 3:

Don't Mess with the Carter Boys